Kaya had to do a double take.

The man jumping out of the orange-and-black safari vehicle and striding toward her had an air about him that she hadn't witnessed before, not least because of the military-style boots, the off-white safari trousers tucked into them and the black T-shirt stretched across a broad muscled chest.

This was pure South African magnificence.

He took her suitcase in one big hand and extended the other to greet her, and she noticed the way his shaved head gleamed in the headlights below a trace of jet-black regrowth, the way his sharp cheekbones and strong jawline turned him into some kind of living, breathing sculpture.

"Kaya?" he said, interrupting her thoughts. It wasn't often she was thrown off her course of thoughts around new men—which usually went something like *He's very good-looking, but he probably can't be trusted.*

"Hey, Kaya? Good to meet you. I'm Arno."

Kaya stared. This was Arno Nkosi? The founder of the volunteer program at the Lindiwe Health Foundation, which was set to be her place of employment for the next six months?

D0381304

Dear Reader,

Years ago, I was flown to Cape Town for a weekend by an extravagant ex-boyfriend—which seems like a distant dream now! The one thing I remember most about that time is the sunsets. The sky at night was on fire, just miles and miles of hot red waves that looked like burning embers on the mountaintops. It was mesmerizing!

Then, of course, there were the vineyards. Some of the most beautiful wineries in the world, to be appreciated tipsy or sober. While the ex didn't last, the memories did, and I'm so glad to be able to bring them into this book. Please enjoy this story of a growing love among the sunsets and safaris of South Africa. Best enjoyed with a Pinotage, of course.

Becky

SOUTH AFRICAN
ESCAPE TO HEAL HER

———

BECKY WICKS

HARLEQUIN

MEDICAL
ROMANCE

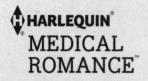

HARLEQUIN®
MEDICAL ROMANCE™

Recycling programs for this product may not exist in your area.

ISBN-13: 978-1-335-73787-8

South African Escape to Heal Her

Copyright © 2023 by Becky Wicks

Harlequin Enterprises ULC
22 Adelaide St. West, 41st Floor
Toronto, Ontario M5H 4E3, Canada
www.Harlequin.com

Printed in U.S.A.

Born in the UK, **Becky Wicks** has suffered interminable wanderlust from an early age. She's lived and worked all over the world, from London to Dubai, Sydney, Bali, New York City and Amsterdam. She's written for the likes of *GQ*, *Hello!*, *Fabulous* and *Time Out*, a host of YA romance, plus three travel memoirs—*Burqalicious*, *Balilicious* and *Latinalicious* (HarperCollins Australia). Now she blends travel with romance for Harlequin and loves every minute! Tweet her @bex_wicks and subscribe at beckywicks.com.

Books by Becky Wicks

Harlequin Medical Romance

Tempted by Her Hot-Shot Doc
From Doctor to Daddy
Enticed by Her Island Billionaire
Falling Again for the Animal Whisperer
Fling with the Children's Heart Doctor
White Christmas with Her Millionaire Doc
A Princess in Naples
The Vet's Escape to Paradise
Highland Fling with Her Best Friend

Visit the Author Profile page at Harlequin.com.

Dedicated to The One Who Took Me To Cape Town,
and all the sunsets we shared.

Praise for
Becky Wicks

"Absolutely entertaining, fast-paced and a story
I couldn't put down.... Overall, Ms. Wicks has
delivered a wonderful read in this book where the
chemistry between this couple was strong; the
romance was delightful and special."
—*Harlequin Junkie* on *From Doctor to Daddy*

CHAPTER ONE

ARNO NKOSI KEPT one hand on the wheel of the Jeep and ran the other lovingly through the thick, coarse fur around Tande's neck. A night drive across the expansive game reserve with all its bullfrog songs and wildlife surprises was an experience his lioness had loved, ever since he'd found her as a lost cub on a sandy roadside, four years ago. Arno assumed Tande's mother had been shot. Or maybe she'd perished in the blade-sharp jaws of a crocodile—who could say?

In this part of the Limpopo Province, in what they called the Safari Capital of South Africa, anything could happen. Which was precisely why he was driving faster than he normally would towards his new volunteer recruit.

A certain Kaya Van der Bijl had flown in from her native Netherlands to work for him and *with* him, but she'd somehow managed to take the wrong bus from Cape Town. Luckily she was waiting for him right now at his friend Rai's small guest resort, which was the closest place he could think of to send her from the bus stop in a pinch. Rai had gone to get her, being the great family friend he was, and had been for a long time, since even *before* the fire...

Arno let a gush of air from his nostrils, turning off all thoughts of the fire before they could burn him, as usual, and sped up towards the game reserve gates. Dutch-born doctor Kaya was out of harm's way, but it did not sit well with Arno that a woman was waiting for him alone in a strange new place, when she should be unpacking with the other volunteers already.

He hoped the staff quarters would be comfy enough. He'd had the basic huts built at the Thabisa Game Reserve to host the steady stream of medical professionals who came to volunteer for six months, sometimes more, with the pioneering healthcare infrastructure project he'd also built—so to speak—from the ground up. He swelled with pride every time someone praised the Lindiwe Health Foundation but in no way could he take *all* the credit. These volunteers made it the success it had been for the last decade, and he needed them safe, comfortable, well fed and well rested, alert and ready to help people in the surrounding communities. Not stranded fifty miles away.

Arno slowed the vehicle, noting Tande's ears

flatten. If a lioness cohort was good for anything, it was for sensing people and animals way before they hit the glare of a handheld spotlight, or his headlights. He watched her long whiskers twitch, and the way she held her nose to the wind. She could be sensing a jackal. It could even be a giraffe. The Thabisa Game Reserve was more alive at night than in the day; you never knew what you might come across, chomping away on a nocturnal feast.

Arno squinted, scanned the darkness ahead for the gleaming green eyes of an impala or a skittish rhino, either of which they would do best to avoid. His mouth flickered with a smile as two snuffling bush pigs looked up in alarm, then darted out of the spotlights.

'Hey, guys,' he muttered at them, drawing to a stop at the gates and turning to Tande.

'They're lucky you've eaten already, huh, girl?' he muttered, and Tande, as if on cue, excused herself from the Jeep by way of leaping gracefully over the door, and padded off into the night. Somehow, she always knew when to make her exit; when Arno was safe from all other wildlife in the reserve, and when *she* could remain well out of sight and reach from whatever might lurk outside.

Of course, he had a gun at hand always, plus a tranquilliser kit and enough antivenom to kill a superhero's arch-enemy, but still. Sometimes it wasn't even the animals you had to be afraid of, he thought ruefully, and the flames roared back into his memory, as bright and loud and ferocious as they were when they tore through the restaurant, twenty years ago.

Back when he was too busy pouring liquor down his throat with his buddies to be home, where he should have been.

He should really call Mama back, he thought suddenly.

Maybe later.

Arno bobbed his head at Mikal, who opened the gate from his protective booth, ushering him on through to the main road. His rammed schedule was just an excuse. It just made his guts squirm, knowing the conversation he'd been putting off for years was always lingering unspoken between them.

Mama never talked about the miscarriage, caused by the carbon monoxide in the smoke, but he still thought about it, every single day. A little brother for Arno she'd never seen coming! A miracle, she'd said. Mama got labelled a geriatric, because she'd had Arno at twenty-two, then fallen pregnant again aged forty. She'd even named her little miracle—Kung, short for Kungawo.

The day he learned they'd lost Kung was still

one of the most vivid memories of his life so far. Mama would be a proud mother of two right now, if he'd only been there when the fire broke out, woken her up from her nap, as he had said he would…

Damn, Arno, focus.

It was twenty goddam years ago, he'd done so much since then. Started a foundation, launched a medical centre, helped to save a thousand lives in the surrounding villages. Reared a frightened little animal from a lion cub to a full-grown lioness, refused even a drop of alcohol…which most people thought strange, considering the family wine empire. But his father's voice was still clear as day, even two whole decades later, blaming him in a moment of rage. Calling him out for not being there; which he'd had every right to. The whole thing had been stalking him like a lion all these years.

He only hoped his waiting volunteer wasn't some frightened little animal; this wasn't exactly work for the weak. Kaya Van der Bijl had seemed pretty tough on the voice call, he mused. She'd talked about her qualifications a lot. Her long years of studying to become a doctor, and the requisite year of training in a Dutch hospital— that was all certainly impressive. As if all that meant a damn thing if she wound up freezing in the face of a flesh wound inflicted on a human by an angry animal.

Or showed up ten minutes too late to a fire.

Arno forged ahead into the night, praying there wouldn't be anything too dramatic to scare Kaya and the other volunteers off. At least not *this* week.

Kaya Van der Bijl had to do a double take. The man jumping out of the orange and black safari vehicle in a cloud of dust and striding towards her now had an air about him that she certainly hadn't witnessed before, not least because of the military-style boots, and the off-white safari trousers tucked into them, and the black T-shirt stretched across a broad muscled chest. This was not Amsterdam attire, not by any stretch of the imagination.

This was pure South African magnificence.

He took her overstuffed suitcase in one big hand and extended the other to greet her, and she noticed the way his shaved head gleamed in the headlights below a trace of jet-black regrowth; the way his sharp cheekbones and strong jawline served to turn him into some kind of living, breathing sculpture. The moonlight just made him seem like a magical creature, born from the wild plains all around them.

'Kaya?' he said, interrupting her thoughts.

It wasn't often she was thrown off her usual course of thoughts around new men—which usually went something like, *Yes, brain, he's very good-looking, but he probably can't be trusted.*

'Hey, Kaya? Good to meet you, I'm Arno. Took the wrong bus, did you?'

Kaya stared. This was Arno Nkosi? The chief medical manager and founder of the volunteer programme at the Lindiwe Health Foundation, which was set to be her place of employment for the next six months? She'd seen a couple of photos of him on the website, but nothing up close... as he was now.

He was partly amused, partly annoyed and trying not to let it show, she observed, forcing her shoulders back and telling her eyes not to rove over his bulging forearms as she smoothed down her white linen dress. Being astute was her speciality, she'd made it that way after everything she was trying to leave far behind her in Amsterdam. Her instincts were primed, all ready to mistrust this strapping man, who was leading her towards the safari four-by-four with the name of the resort they were headed for on the side of it—*Thabisa Game Reserve.*

She was already late for unpacking hour in the promised 'rustic yet scenic' staff quarters she'd be staying at on a self-catering basis. Suddenly she thought less about not trusting him, and hoped he didn't think less of her for missing the bus. They'd be working closely together.

Lifting her bag effortlessly over the side of the Jeep, despite the array of vacuum-sealed bags she'd stuffed inside to hide the actual bulk of her belongings, Arno nodded in the direction of the three steps she had to climb to take her seat. She was careful to jump up without letting her dress rise too high.

The leather seat felt thin and she wasn't entirely sure it had much in the way of suspension, but hey, she was here in South Africa, the place of her mother's birth. And where she was headed, she wasn't exactly expecting luxury.

'Sorry I missed the bus,' she heard herself saying when Arno had exchanged a quick goodbye with the guy he'd apparently sent to rescue her from the bus stop. He must know everyone around here.

'It happens,' Arno replied in a manner that suggested it didn't usually happen and should not have happened tonight. She cringed internally as they swung out of the quaint guest house's driveway. His hands looked big and strong on the steering wheel.

'Did you have to drive very far to come and get me?' she asked, wondering how many lives he'd saved with those two big hands. 'I know we're surrounded by game parks so I wasn't sure if there's a shortcut you might have.'

'The only shortcut is through the game park,' he said. 'The one where you'll be staying. It's gated and guarded like they all are, but you wouldn't want to walk it. Not unless you want a face-off with a wild pig. Or a rhino.'

'How often does that happen?'

'More often than you'd think.'

She caught his lips curl slightly and wondered if he was joking, and also if she'd sounded naive talking about shortcuts. She had been quite distracted at the airport, noticing all the things her mother had been talking about for years—the wide welcoming smiles, the colourful clothes, the African trinkets shining from the tourist stalls. No wonder she'd taken the wrong bus. She'd finally made it to her mother's birthplace. She'd always been curious about this side of her family but never enough to actually come here. Scrap that, had she just made herself too busy, or been too afraid? Since the attack, she hadn't exactly been chomping at the bit to leap out of her comfort zone. She was only just now realising she'd probably wasted some of the best years of her life—well, no more!

'So, this is your first time here?' Arno was looking at her sideways, as if he'd read her mind.

'To South Africa? Yes. But I've been dreaming about it for years,' she replied, unable to hide the excitement in her voice, or the urge to study him closer while he was driving. The contrast between her mocha skin and his sun-kissed whiteness was striking, even in the low light. They didn't make male specimens like Arno where she'd grown up in the Netherlands—the men were tall enough but, to her, they all looked kind of the same. Not that she'd noticed any of them with romance in mind since the attack, or since Pieter…

Nope. He was not allowed into her thoughts any more, not here, the cheater.

'It's not a vacation,' Arno replied, coolly, watching the road. Kaya straightened her back in the bumpy seat and gripped the side handlebar. They were speeding down a dirt track now. The lights from the guest house were a mere glow behind them.

'I'm not expecting a holiday. I just meant my mother is from Cape Town, and I've always wanted to see the country she left when she moved to the Netherlands. That's where my dad's from, but they met here.'

'Do you have siblings?' he asked, seemingly interested.

'I have one younger brother,' she replied. 'Daan is three years younger than me, he's twenty-four. He's studying architecture.'

'Younger brother, huh?'

She nodded. 'We're quite close. Do *you* have siblings?'

A furrow appeared between Arno's eyebrows as he looked dead ahead over the steering wheel. 'Nope. Just me.'

The inkling of something like anger lingering beneath his words caught her off guard. On instinct she searched the road ahead for something blocking their path, or anything that might have caused 'that look', but there was nothing.

Was she talking too much? Kaya smoothed her dress hoping it wasn't sweaty, and wondered if her English was as good as everyone said it was. Everyone spoke English at home, as much as they did Dutch, but she was aware of her own accent now, as much as she was aware of Arno's.

His South African lilt sent his words up at the ends in little sing-song flourishes. She quite enjoyed it. But now he was simply frowning at the windshield.

What was he—late thirties? He looked at least a decade older than her. He'd done some pretty incredible things in Limpopo, she thought, starting with founding and recruiting new volunteers every six months to assist with important medical rounds and much-needed treatments in the local communities. The nearest town of Hoedspruit was surrounded by game reserves, and therefore called the Safari Capital of South Africa. This position, for the next six months, could mean some difficult tasks, out in potentially dangerous places. She wondered if he was concerned that she wouldn't be up for the task.

Usually she'd be wary of all this herself. Not because she felt she was lacking in qualifications or experience—she most certainly was not. But because…well…

Kaya glanced his way; the old nemesis of distrust flaring up against her will. Was this Arno a man she could be alone with? He might be a man of few words, but then, he *was* someone everyone knew, she reminded herself. He'd done more in his years as a doctor and surgeon than most people half his age—if he was indeed in his late thirties, as opposed to her twenty-seven years.

That didn't mean she hadn't conquered enough on her own since dragging herself up from rock bottom, she mused, watching the row of thick bushes spike towards the sky along the roadside. Her poor parents, while happy she was here doing something to help put the past behind her, were apprehensive. Close as they were, they knew she wasn't totally over the assault, not by a long shot. The man still pounced on her in her dreams every now and then; sometimes they were back in the park where it happened three years ago. Sometimes they were in a darkened vault or, worse, her bedroom, where she'd holed up for months afterwards at her parents' house.

Inhaling a lungful of dusty air, she reminded herself in the side mirror that this was a chance at a new start, a new beginning.

'I noticed your name, Kaya, means *restful place* in Zulu,' Arno said now, thoughtfully. 'Interesting, considering you chose a profession that doesn't offer much rest.'

'What?' His observation broke into her daydream.

'Still, I can't see you in a library,' he continued, 'or an ashram. Not if your résumé is anything to go by.'

Kaya laughed nervously. Having someone she barely knew admitting to thinking about her and her history felt a little uncomfortable. But he was her mentor and employer, so, of course, he'd have some questions. And she'd do well to try and at least seem open. Something in his eyes as he looked at her sideways had her nerves rewiring the whole way up her arms.

'What do you do for fun?' he asked now.

That was an interesting question she didn't quite know how to answer. There hadn't been much fun for her, for a while.

'I've done Pilates for a while. Kickboxing too,' she replied carefully. 'And you know how the Dutch love a peaceful bike ride.'

Arno laughed. A nice laugh. A laugh she wanted to hear more of, even though it administered a sharp shot of self-loathing that calmed her hummingbird heartbeat in a flash. How was Arno to know she still took the bus everywhere at night, instead of hopping back on her bike, as the Dutch did by default?

The ability to go anywhere alone after dark had abandoned her long ago. What if another faceless male vulture tried to steal her dignity, along with her belongings, like *that* guy...the one who got away? The one who had never been caught.

She hadn't been able to prove a thing. The assault and the injustice had ruled everything for years, ruined her relationship. Pieter wound up cheating, saying he was forced to, because she wouldn't let him near her, but could he really blame her after having a stranger almost rape her in a park? Just the smallest touch, or brush against her arm in a crowd, by anyone, not just him, had flooded her with panic and self-loathing.

She only hoped no one else came along and tried the same thing with her. Maybe this time they'd succeed in getting further than a handful of her breasts and a feel of her...

No, God, no...

'You OK?' Arno was looking at her in concern

now and she drew her chin to her chest. 'I know it all probably looks a little different from what you're used to, and getting the wrong bus might have thrown you, but no harm will come to you on my watch. I can *promise* you that.'

Kaya turned to look at him. His last statement...that had sounded serious. As if he knew what she'd been through to get here—as if he *possibly* could.

'That's good to know. And thanks, I'm fine,' she replied, noting how her heart was thudding wildly again in her chest, like a satellite that for years had been floating silently in space, and was finally now picking up a signal.

CHAPTER TWO

ARNO WAVED AT Mikal again as the guard opened the gates to Thabisa Game Reserve. He saw him take a long look at Kaya, before peering through the window and resting his arms on the frame with his usual wide, toothy grin. 'Welcome to Thabisa, young lady. I see you're getting the special treatment already, being collected by the boss.'

'You came out of nowhere!'

Kaya sounded panicked. She drew a sharp breath and recoiled in her seat, as if she couldn't get away from Mikal fast enough. Quickly, sensing her discomfort, Arno left Mikal behind in a cloud of dust, almost as fast as poor Mikal could pull his head back out of the Jeep.

'Mikal is a big guy but he wouldn't hurt a sandfly,' he told her as he rumbled back the way he'd come, towards the resort and its staff quarters. 'Did you see his gun, in the holster? Everyone has one here.'

Kaya looked embarrassed now. His forehead wrinkled with a frown as she released her own forearms from the knot she'd tied herself up in. 'Oh, no, I didn't even see the gun. Sorry, Arno, he just came out of nowhere…sorry.'

'Don't apologise,' he said, feeling a little bad for the way he'd almost reprimanded her before, when he said this wasn't a vacation. He realised now that maybe his tone had been a little harsh, and that his defences were up because she was undeniably attractive, and he didn't quite know what to do with that. He wasn't prepared to spend the next six months fighting some attraction to someone he couldn't touch—he was meant to be a professional, a mentor. Not some Romeo, following her with his eyes through every emergency. And there would be emergencies. Distractions weren't welcome, not here.

Then the whole sibling thing had struck a nerve, too…

But really, she hadn't seen the gun? What on earth was so frightening about big, goofy Mikal? Maybe she was just exhausted from the journey.

'You're in a new place,' he offered. 'You're probably also jet-lagged. Let's get you to your new home, shall we?'

Kaya forced a smile verging on wary and kept her eyes on the road ahead. She kept her right hand clasped like a steel vice around the overhead handle, as if she didn't trust his driving either. He always drove safely, but if he didn't go fast he'd never get anywhere; at least, not before it was too late.

Arno slowed the Jeep a little anyway, glancing in her direction, instincts primed. That had been some reaction. What on earth…was she going to be visibly frightened of new people out here, new experiences? That wouldn't get her very far. A muscle in his jaw ticked. A pretty woman like this, with eyes like hers, and flawless, caramel skin like hers, and full heart-shaped movie star lips…she'd do well to keep her wits about her, and not let any ruffled feathers show. Plenty of people could take advantage of that.

He felt his hands clamp harder around the wheel. Kaya was his responsibility now.

'What is that?' Kaya's eyes had popped beside him. Her look drew him from his reverie, which had strangely and rather irritatingly been veering on admitting to himself that she was possibly the prettiest volunteer who'd shown up here in a long time.

'What is what?' he followed, clearing his throat, but no sooner had the words left his mouth than the shadow of a figure he knew well drew up alongside the Jeep. *Tande*.

Her fur was a blaze of white in the moonlight. The glint of her cat eyes as she streaked across their path just ahead made Kaya let out a shriek. 'A lion! Arno, it's a lion, hurry up, we need to…'

He stopped the Jeep. 'It's OK.' Arno put a hand to Kaya's shoulder, looked towards Tande, who'd stopped to eye them both up through the windshield. 'You're about to meet a friend of mine. Just stay calm.'

'A…friend of yours?'

He pressed a finger to his lips. 'Calm. OK? Trust me. Do you trust me?'

A moment passed between them. Kaya's obsidian eyes burned into his as she nodded mutely, her expression flickering between hope and caution. Trusting him wasn't coming easily, he could tell. Basic instinct told him it went beyond Mikal and the lioness just outside, and his mind spun suddenly—who was this woman and why was she really here?

He removed his hand from her arm, just as Tande leaped gracefully onto the bonnet of the Jeep and started licking her paws like a giant house cat who'd been looking for a warm place to sit. He could tell Kaya was biting her cheeks, trying not to make a sound. This time he definitely did not blame her for startling, but they were going to meet eventually, so now was as good a time as any.

'Tande is a rescue,' he explained, opening the door slightly. 'I found her as a cub. She just likes to hang out, that's all.' He jumped to the dusty ground, shutting the door behind him, protecting Kaya. Tande had never hurt anyone, but she was still a wild creature and she could sense fear in strangers.

His boots shook up more dust on the dry moonlit ground. Every stride echoed through the night, and he felt Kaya watching him as Tande jumped from the Jeep to greet him. He ran his hands across her head and ears, letting her nuzzle him, showing Kaya she could be trusted. Then he held out his hand to her.

He half expected her to flat-out refuse to participate in this introduction, but Kaya obliged, if tentatively, crossing to him slowly and taking his outstretched hand. He used his other hand to rub Tande's ears, then gently placed Kaya's palm to her fur, encouraging her to take over, noting the fuzzy sensation that took over and blurred the world around them at her touch.

'I wouldn't let you, if it wasn't safe,' he said, looking into her eyes, and relief washed over her features as she started to run a hand lightly over the lioness's head.

Pure elation crossed her face in the headlights and Arno found himself lost a second, dazzled by the broad smile—this was the first he'd seen of it, and she was truly stunning. South African and Dutch, huh, he mused. The two made for a good mix.

As if watching the moment from above, he observed the fact that he was actually sharing the magic that was Tande under the moon with a woman he'd just met, and how weirdly calm he felt about that. This had never happened before.

'She's beautiful,' Kaya breathed, and he studied the smoothness of her mocha skin up close, the depths in her eyes. The way her dress nipped in around her middle, enhancing her small waist and toned upper arms.

'She is,' he agreed.

'Tande…that means teeth, in Dutch,' Kaya observed as Tande decided she'd had enough petting for one night and turned her back on them slowly, her attention switching to some distant noise that they as mere humans couldn't hear. 'I suppose that fits. Aren't you ever scared?'

'Of Tande?' he answered.

'No, of the dentist. Of course, Tande!'

He shrugged. 'I've known fear,' he admitted, picturing the moment he had arrived on the driveway to find the flames licking the stone walls of the villa, shattering windows; people screaming, no sight of his pregnant mama. 'It's never been related to my lion.'

Kaya cocked a head at him. 'What kind of fear are we talking about?'

Arno shook his head at the floor. He *could* elaborate on how that fire had taken three of his parents' beloved staff members, and, later, his unborn baby brother. It had dominated the news for a long time, back when the prized family business and the longest running winery in Stellenbosch went up in flames, but they'd only just met. Anyway, he never really talked about it with anyone, let alone a stranger. If he did, he'd have to mention how the miscarriage was *his* fault.

He'd abandoned therapy because not even the long-faced lady with the big, beguiling eyes and irritatingly soft voice could get him to talk about it. It was stuffed down deep under the daily grind where it couldn't get to him. Apart from Bea, the one woman he'd opened his heart to about it all, no one had met Mama Annika. There hadn't been anyone since, but he'd never take another woman home.

What if someone asked the same things Bea had, like why they hadn't redecorated and reopened the restaurant? He'd have to say it was because Mama wanted to keep the memories alive through the blackened walls and fire-tinged beams.

Memories of his brother, who had died because of him.

Bea had left him shortly after learning the truth, five years ago now. She'd wanted to explore other places, and other relationships. He had never found out for sure if she just thought less of him, after learning how he'd let his family down, but he had clearly let Bea down too, somewhere along the way. A year-long relationship, his longest one ever, had just gone up in flames, like everything else. His biggest dread was letting people down, the way he'd let his parents down. God, his father had been so damn angry. The family had never been the same since.

'What kind of fear?' Kaya asked again, eyes narrowed.

'The debilitating kind,' he replied darkly.

'Well, that makes two of us.' Kaya sighed, and Arno detected a deep sadness, at the same time as he became acutely aware that her hand was still in his, even with no lioness to pet or protect her from.

As if realising the same thing, she pulled away and busied her hands with smoothing her hair, eyeing him sideways as Tande padded off. 'But if you say your lion has never eaten anyone...'

'Not that I know of.' He motioned her back to the Jeep, forcing himself not to look at her. They'd be working together; in some tricky situations, no doubt. The last thing he needed was a distraction, but he could have sworn they had just had some kind of *moment*. And what kind of fear was *she* talking about, exactly?

'Do you have many animal friends?' she asked as they bumped along the dirt track. The lights from the resort were just ahead, which for some reason was a relief to him now. 'I mean, should I expect a friendly elephant to climb in next?'

'Maybe just a rhino or two,' he replied, dead-pan, and she huffed a small laugh, looking around her warily. 'I'm kidding, of course,' he continued. 'No one's friends with the rhinos. They love to charge off in the direction you least expect, just to relieve their own boredom and stress. They're unpredictable. Never approach one, ever.'

'I wasn't planning on it.'

His turn to smirk now.

By the time he pulled up outside the staff huts and carried her suitcase diligently to her door, he'd decided there was something dangerously interesting about Kaya Van der Bijl. He'd do best to keep away from her, outside their professional duties. Already she stirred something up in him that reminded him of Bea. Bea had tornadoed into his life, a PR for a wine company who'd come for a safari and slashed her leg on a wire fence. Their romance had been the best year of his life, until it became the worst.

The moment he'd finally opened up about the fire, and told her why it had taken him almost a year to take her home to meet his mother, no thanks to his debilitating guilt over ruining her life, she'd all but disappeared. She was thriving with a new man now, somewhere in Spain, that much he knew. And here he was, single, which was maybe the only way he couldn't disappoint anyone else.

Sometimes he wondered if it had been the wine estate Bea was interested in that whole time, more than him. But either way, no one since had got close enough to break him and they never would if he could help it. Especially not someone he was supposed to be working with!

CHAPTER THREE

'THIS IS BETSY, named by the British volunteer who first drove her out through the gates,' Arno explained, and Kaya watched his bicep rise like a boulder in his white T-shirt as he slapped a hand to the side of the huge truck that was their mobile medical clinic. The bus-sized vehicle had been designed to be driven through the townships around Cape Town, and the local communities in between.

The sunlight streaked across his arms, and she noted the faint line where a watch might have been; the black snake tattoo that curled like some family emblem on his bicep. She didn't usually like tattoos on anyone, not even Pieter when he'd had the initials of his late grandfather inked on his upper arm in memory. But Arno's was hot, she decided, while allowing the fact to sink in that she was literally admiring a man, rather than wanting to run a mile. So strange. But not entirely unwelcome. Maybe it was being so far away from home, away from triggers. The old 'out of sight, out of mind' thing?

'Every doctor that's here is making a huge impact on the health of the surrounding community and to individuals themselves,' Arno was saying now, arms crossed. He was wearing the black military boots again, the same cargo trousers, and a blue T-shirt with the foundation's logo on it—the same as the one she was in, only hers was slim fit.

'As you all know, the Lindiwe Health Foundation's services are varied. There's not one emergency we haven't already dealt with. You're all here because of your individual skills, and because I saw something in each of you during the application process...'

Arno caught her eye then, mid-speech, and dashed his shaved head with one hand. As he continued talking about the last few surgeries he'd done in the well-stocked mobile clinic to the group of five other volunteers she was standing amongst, Kaya realised she was mirroring him, scraping her wild curls back on her hot head, wondering why he made her nervous.

It wasn't the usual nerves she felt around men; as in, it wasn't general disdain or mistrust occupying her brain whenever Arno was near. It was a kind of natural attraction that had fizzled into her conscience in the Jeep last night. Who wouldn't admire this brooding surgeon's looks?

But looks were just surface distractions. She'd been awed speechless by the fact that he'd tamed a lion.

Tande. Wow!

She'd never had a moment like that before, and probably never would again. Not just meeting a real lioness, but letting a guy she'd just met hold her hand throughout the whole experience. It would never have happened normally, but she'd been thrown, numbed almost by the creature's magnificence. And Arno's. What kind of man tamed a wild lion from a cub to the creature she'd met last night? Someone special, for sure.

Not that she was here to pet the wildlife...or wonder what made Arno Nkosi tick. She was here to work.

Except, she couldn't *help* wondering what made him tick. There had been a moment between them, she was certain, because she never had 'moments' with men. What debilitating fear had *he* known? Whatever it was, she recognised a kindred spirit when she saw one.

Obviously, she had no desire at all to elaborate further on her own experience, spending three whole years being afraid to cycle through a stupid park thanks to one drunk, entitled arsehole. But how could she not want to know what he'd gone through himself, what caused that look on his face—so distant, as though he'd gone someplace else in his head, somewhere bad?

Was he attacked by the rhinos he'd warned her about? Did he fight a snake after it bit him, thus inciting his desire for the tattoo? Maybe she shouldn't be thinking about it so much…

'He's so sexy, don't you think?'

Kaya was pulled from her reverie by the whisper of a volunteer next to her; a short, pale-skinned lady from Australia in a red hat called Kimberley. Kaya kept a straight face, refused to turn to her. Instead, she shrugged as her cheeks flushed.

'You couldn't keep your eyes off him at breakfast. I saw you.' Kimberley grinned and nudged her. 'Don't worry, who wouldn't think that?'

Kaya flinched. Touching her was unnecessary—no one touched her if she could help it. Well, no one but Arno last night, which she was still processing. The fact that she'd let him was still a surprise, lioness or no lioness. And anyway, she hadn't been staring at Arno over breakfast.

Had she?

Arno was still talking. 'You'll be getting plenty of hands-on and practical experience, all of you. A lot of our rural doctors who do come and work here end up leaving a lot more confident in their skills, and in their training…'

Her eyes caught his again. *Hands-on* didn't sound so bad. She straightened up, feigning a confidence she didn't feel in his line of vision. *He* wasn't to know she'd lacked confidence of sorts since the assault, or that she was here to try and prove to herself that she could face life without fear again, explore new places without being afraid of her own shadow, and gain back some of the confidence that had pretty much defined her before that night in the park.

Kimberley nudged her again and she frowned, moving away. OK, so maybe she had been watching Arno at breakfast, regretting the way she'd recoiled from that guy at the gate on the way into the resort in front of him—the one who'd stuck his head in the window out of nowhere and given her a fright. She hadn't even noticed the gun. He'd just shown up out of nowhere; something that was bound to trigger her.

While wishing—again—that she hadn't made quite such a scene in the Jeep, she'd counted two slices of toast at breakfast, two hard-boiled eggs and three rings of pineapple on his plate. Then, when he'd sat down opposite her and eaten in silence, she'd counted the freckles that formed a jagged constellation on his left forearm— seven—and the tiny scales on the snake tattoo—

twenty-eight—and allowed herself to ask him if he had any more tattoos.

He'd replied no, and that had been the extent of their exchange, although his piercing slate-blue gaze had lingered on hers until she'd pulled her eyes away.

He'd sprung up after that, as if he was far too busy to be eating breakfast, let alone discussing tattoos with her, and she'd found herself watching him stride purposefully towards the mesh mosquito-proof door, until he'd disappeared from view.

'I need a volunteer,' he said now. Without missing a beat, Kaya shot up her hand. What she was volunteering for, she had no idea, but she was going to at least come across as a professional, starting now.

Arno beckoned her towards him. 'Great, Kaya,' he said. 'You'll be coming with me on our first round—we only need the two of us where we're going. The rest of you five can go with Dr Zula in Betsy here and start on the PLH Project.'

He turned to her and scanned her eyes. 'That's the Positive Lifestyle Habits Project—volunteers can work with small groups to deliver information on basic health, lifestyle and nutrition. I think you missed that intro yesterday, because you got here late, but don't worry. You'll catch up.'

Was that a dig for the fact she got on the wrong

bus? Kaya wasn't sure, but she stood taller anyway. 'I read up on this before I came,' she told him, while the others were chatting amongst themselves, boarding the mobile clinic. 'I was thinking maybe we could start a small vegetable garden somewhere that the community can help look after. We can use the harvest for malnourished patients too.'

Arno ran a hand across his chin this time, seemingly running her idea around in his head. 'I love it,' he replied after a moment, and her heart did a little leapfrog.

Before she knew it, Kaya was back in the Jeep and Arno was bumping them back across the reserve, this time in the midday sun.

She squinted through her sunglasses as he explained they were heading to visit some patients who were too sick or impoverished to get to their nearest clinic. They were in a tiny village that not even the mobile clinic could reach, which already made her heart pang with sympathy.

'You'll be helping me with the new TB antigen tests today. There was a recent outbreak in the village where we're going.' He paused and slowed as a zebra wandered into the path and trotted off again. 'All children are supposed to get the BCG vaccine at birth in South Africa, but some slip the net. A high HIV co-infection rate means that in some of these rural, resource-poor areas…'

'I read about it. It's terrible.' She sighed.

'Yes. It is.' He pulled the visor down, shading his face. 'Some of these people already have both tuberculosis and HIV,' he followed. 'It might be a little confronting at first…'

'I can handle it,' she assured him, hoping she could. 'I'm willing to do whatever is needed, Dr…'

'Just Arno is fine,' he asserted, and she noticed how his face softened slightly. 'I'm sure you're up to this. You wouldn't have come here if you weren't, right?'

'Right,' she said, forcing conviction, hoping this wasn't another test of her abilities and confidence.

'I appreciate your idea too, about the garden. Are you green-fingered back home too?'

She shrugged, picturing the patch of tomatoes, courgettes and lettuces she'd tended over the last three years. It had all started as an excuse to disappear from society after the attack.

'I got a little something going on my rooftop in Amsterdam,' she ventured. 'I didn't know how much I would grow to enjoy it. Something about putting your hands in the dirt, in the earth, growing something tangible from nothing under the sun.'

'You get sun there?' He cocked an eyebrow.

'Sometimes.'

He nodded, a rueful smile hovering on his lips. 'Growing something tangible from nothing under the sun. Sounds like something my mama would say, Kaya.'

'Why did you start the foundation?' she asked him now, keen to continue the conversation, and also registering the way her name sounded from his mouth, how it made her feel as if he'd grabbed her insides with his big hands and twisted them ever so slightly into brand-new positions, every single one attuned to his intonations.

'It's a good feeling, knowing you're making a difference to someone's life,' he replied. 'Besides, I didn't think the wine business was for me.'

Kaya studied his taut jawline. 'Wine business?'

'My whole family is in the wine business,' he said. 'You hadn't heard?'

'*Should* I have heard?'

The moment she said it, the faintest recollection of a gold-embossed wine label flashed to the front of her memory bank. 'Oh… Nkosi Valley wine… I don't drink, haven't for years but, now that you mention it, I've seen it. That's your family?'

He nodded sagely. 'I don't drink either,' he

told her, as visions of a family-run vineyard enchanted her suddenly. She didn't know much about the world of wine but surely wine producers around this region were rich, so Arno must have come from money. He could have done anything, but he'd chosen to help others. Her admiration for him ratcheted up another notch.

'When was the last time you had a drink?' she asked, wondering if it was as long ago as her. She hadn't touched a drop since the assault three years ago. Maybe if she hadn't been tipsy following her expat friend's birthday shenanigans at an Irish pub in the Red Light District she would've been more aware of her surroundings, maybe veered left at the lights instead of right into the park and into the hands of…him.

'Haven't touched a drop since I was eighteen years old,' Arno answered.

'Most people don't start till then,' she observed.

'I started too early. *Big* mistake.'

'Too early? How early is too early?'

'Early enough to make me late for something way more important. So tell me, what kind of music are you into, over in the Netherlands?'

Without leaving room for her answer, he reached for the dial on the dash and, in seconds, music blasted through the vehicle, signalling the end of their conversation. Kaya set her gaze upon the jagged trees outside the window. It felt a lot as if he'd been about to tell her something he deemed incredibly important, and then decided not to.

Oh, well, everyone had their secrets, she supposed. Especially her. Except the most puzzling thing was happening to her now. The more Arno talked, the more she was finding herself drawn to him…wondering things about him. She'd do well not to get too personal in any further discussions.

Gosh, she'd die if he knew some of the things *she* kept hidden…like the fact that Pieter started seeing someone else behind her back because she was, in his words, 'frigid and cold', but he 'didn't want to hurt her more by breaking things off'—coward.

Last night was the first time since that awful night when she'd actually let a man she didn't know take her hand. Why she had let Arno, why he was getting to her after so long of trying to forget all men existed, was not only interesting, it was a little jarring too. The thought of letting anyone get that close again, close enough to hurt her, was…well, terrifying.

CHAPTER FOUR

THE CHILDREN DESCENDED on them, the moment they pulled up in the Jeep. They always did. The little ones especially expected crayons and sweets, although Arno never brought the sweets. 'Dentistry is not what it is in the western world,' he explained, when Kaya asked why he hadn't brought the candy hearts they were asking for.

Arno watched her eyes widen and narrow in shock and despair as she took in the full extent of life in this tiny community, hidden from the world, an hour's drive from the resort in a remote valley. The mountainous backdrop promised safaris and breweries and wineries beyond, a plethora of luxurious modern charms, none of which existed here.

'This is where they live?' Kaya whispered to him, gesturing to the row of bleak-looking thatch-roofed huts stitched together with woven branches, mud and dried cow dung. Two pigs that looked far too skinny were snuffling around a wire-fence enclosure, where several chickens pecked at the ground.

He nodded sagely. 'They're pretty self-sufficient, and they share what they have,' he said. 'But I know they'll get a lot out of your garden.'

'Where should we build the structure for that?' Kaya swung around, bumping into him, making him drop the box of tests he'd just pulled from the back seat. His heart slammed into top gear at her proximity as her scent washed over him. 'Sorry, sorry,' she said quickly as she sprang away from him, then immediately bumped into his arm again as she tried to help pick it up.

'It's OK,' he assured her, collecting the fallen box and brushing the mud off the bottom with his hand. 'It's dirty work out here; as long as what's inside it is kept clean, we're good.'

Kaya rubbed her arm self-consciously where she'd knocked him, and he caught the same haunted look in her eyes that he'd seen yesterday, when she'd admitted she knew fear, as he did. Things were falling into place, he thought to himself. Kaya had a thing about physical contact. The way she'd reacted with Mikal at the gates to Thabisa was one thing, but what about this morning? He wasn't born yesterday. That Australian volunteer, Kimberley, had been whispering about him, but Kaya was having none of it. Not only did she keep her mouth shut, which he respected, she'd practically built a wall between them when Kimberley prodded and nudged her.

His animal instincts were primed; something must have happened to make her so guarded. Probably something bad.

A strange kind of need to protect her took a hold of him, more powerful than yesterday. And instantly jarring—he hadn't felt this way since he'd seen Bea lying bloodied by that fence and raced to help her, determined, as he had been every day since that fire, not to let a person who needed him down. Why Kaya was summoning those same feelings he almost didn't want to contemplate; she'd be leaving soon, as Bea had, whether she knew his family secrets or not.

A burst of laughter made them turn. Two little girls were climbing into the Jeep, pretending to steer it, and he let them. 'They're always so grateful for everything they have,' he said to Kaya, retrieving another box from the back seat and sidestepping around her, wary now of getting too close to her.

He opened the back to retrieve a trellis table and foldable chairs and set them apart. This was the extent of their 'clinic' out here, but they had the new batch of antigen tests they needed and now he had Kaya, and that was all that mattered.

Two barefooted kids dressed in scruffy football shirts and shorts were digging ferociously with plastic shovels over by a makeshift cow-shed. He watched Kaya wander over to them.

'What are you digging?' he heard her ask as he stuck the table legs firmly into the mud in front of the Jeep.

'Fossils,' they told her in unison.

'Fossils? Out here?' she replied, getting to her haunches to inspect something they'd dug up.

'You'd be surprised,' he called over, admiring the curve of her hips in her khaki shorts, and the way that the simple white T-shirt rendered the whole of Kaya the kind of untouchable that could cause a sleepless night if he dwelled on it too long. 'Indigenous habitants left a lot for these guys to unearth. They can sell what they find, so they never stop looking.'

Kaya smiled, touched a hand to the head of one of the boys, and then crossed her arms as she walked back to help him set up, giving him the chance to admire her again with the sun glinting off her mocha skin and wild raven curls.

It wasn't just her looks, though, he considered again as she fetched a box of vials and made small talk with another curious child.

He hadn't been able to stop thinking about that moment with Tande yesterday. Maybe that was what had led him to sit opposite her at breakfast. He'd thought better of it and left the dining hall shortly after, biting back his questions; what was the point of getting personal with a volunteer? That would lead nowhere and, besides, he wasn't exactly the type to invite intimacy in. That always led to questions about…everything…

No, thanks. He had enough on his plate without twisting knives into old wounds.

But never had he allowed a stranger that close to his lioness so soon—not because he didn't trust Tande, of course. He just didn't want to freak anyone out by initiating contact. Kaya had been calm and gentle and Tande had responded. She hadn't padded off straight away as she usually would. He admired a woman who could admire his lioness, but there was something about her.

Maybe it was the haunted look in her eyes he caught every now and then, the hint of a troubled past that made her so…attractive. Now *that* he could relate to, he thought disparagingly, along with the need to escape every now and then.

A little boy no older than four or five was tugging at Kaya's sleeve already and to her credit she didn't even wince at the muddy streak that was left behind. 'Can I go first?' the child asked her, placing his forearm flat on the table, even before she'd sat down.

'You want to be the first to be tested?' She smiled. 'You're one brave boy.'

'I'm not scared of blood,' he told her proudly,

and she laughed, right before the kid regaled a story about helping his father catch, then carve up one of the chickens. Then he said, 'I think I have TB. I'm very tired all the time. I sweat in the night.'

Kaya shot him a sideways look and Arno felt his brows meet in the middle. It wasn't uncommon for kids to diagnose themselves; they saw enough cases to know the signs.

'We'll get you tested, buddy, and if you do have it, we'll get you treatment, don't worry.'

Arno ripped the tape off one of the boxes he'd put on the trellis table. 'These tests are a new alternative to the regular tuberculin skin test,' he told her, sliding a box her way, and placing a box of vials in between them as she took a seat. 'More cost-effective for the foundation, and more accurate.'

'Well, that's always a good thing,' she replied, pushing her hair from her face and eyeing the giant grey resident elephant who'd just plodded into view, led by her keeper.

'That's Alma,' he told her as the huge creature flapped her ears free of pesky flies and sent fresh dust swirling their way. 'One of the guys here rescued her years ago. She pays her way now, pulling timber, giving kids a ride to school. Been through the wars, but I think she's happy here.'

It was getting hotter by the minute, and as

Kaya watched the elephant plod past out of view again, with a look of total enchantment on her face, he found himself wondering if she'd applied sunscreen—the last thing he needed was for her to burn on day one. It was disconcerting how much he was thinking about her already, he realised.

He watched as she rubbed the boy's arm with alcohol and pushed the needle bevel into his skin. Sure enough, the boy didn't even flinch, though an interested circle of faces had gathered, and some of the girls were squealing, not sure what to think.

Arno filled in the labels on the vials, and, along with Kaya, instructed those just tested to avoid scratching or rubbing their arms. The first young boy, who seemed to take a liking to Kaya, lingered as she tested his friends. Worryingly, he'd started to cough, and Arno hoped it wasn't another case of TB, rather another case of a kid breathing in too much dirt, and not eating enough vegetables. He caught Kaya's concerned glance and lowered his voice again, reading her mind. 'We'll have all the results back from the lab in a few days,' he told her.

Within thirty minutes they'd effectively tested everyone who hadn't been tested last time he visited this village, but their mission wasn't over.

* * *

Kaya *was* a little conflicted, if she was honest. The little mud hut they were standing in now wouldn't have even held up as a garden shed where she was from, but the little bony lady Arno called Mama Imka, lying on the thin mattress on the ground was still looking up at her with a sparkle in her eyes.

And what was in all these jars? she thought, noting the haphazard array of glass containers along the cake-like brown walls. So many jars and candles, stacked up in the subdued light bleeding in from the doorway.

'She's a Sangoma. A fortune teller,' Arno explained, seeing her puzzled stare.

'Really?' Kaya felt her eyes widen. She half expected Arno to laugh or roll his eyes her way on the sly—a man of science and medicine didn't believe in all that, did he? But he seemed deadly serious.

'Those are Mama Imka's tools,' he told her, signalling for her to pass him the medical box she'd carried inside. 'Two different worlds, huh?'

The children from outside were crowded around the door, as if they couldn't get enough of watching her and Arno. Or maybe they were wishing their village fortune teller better? She held up a hand at them, noting their muddy feet in the dirt. Different worlds indeed.

'How are you feeling today?' Arno asked the sixty-something lady kindly, crouching to her side. Kaya watched how gentle he was as he rested a hand on her thin, brittle fingers.

'I'm grateful you're here for the others,' she responded, sucking in a breath and flicking her gaze to her again. 'Although you know, and *I* know, what will come for me.'

'Do we?' He smirked, squeezing her fingers. 'I wish you'd accept that your meds are helping, Mama. You're looking better than last week.'

'My dear boy, medicine can only do so much when fate has dealt its cards.'

'Well, let's just keep following doctor's orders anyway, OK?' he said sternly, yet with a stroke of fondness for her that melted Kaya's heart.

Mama Imka sighed and dropped her head against a lumpy-looking pillow. 'As you wish.'

Kaya crouched beside Arno, brushing his arm again accidentally, noting how her body didn't bristle like a frightened cat's at his closeness. Why did even touching him by accident feel different from when she'd brushed anyone else by accident over the last few years? Instead of shooting flashbacks of the assault through her, she felt something like…adrenaline? Excitement?

Maybe it was just being here, with this intriguing woman, she told herself. It wouldn't do to develop a crush on her mentor; besides, it was likely he was around ten years older than her. Completely out of her league in all respects. She hadn't been herself enough to like a guy for years, and she was damned if she'd start now with someone she couldn't even have!

'I'm Kaya. We're here to do your monthly blood test,' she said, noting how the woman's arm was adorned with more beaded bracelets than she could count. Her lips were stained red from some kind of plant or natural dye, she could tell. In fact, she did look quite well considering she was suffering both TB and HIV.

Arno had explained outside how the NGO the foundation worked with provided all TB medications, laboratory testing, X-rays and in-patient care, but it was their job to visit these infected patients weekly and provide injections and support, monitor adverse events, and educate them and their family members in how best to control infection. She hoped the education made as much of a difference as the medications. Already the stench of dirt and animals was making her eyes water.

She watched Arno take the blood test, and then he allowed her to do the sputum culture—testing for infection in the lady's lungs. Mama Imka watched them both intently as they worked, adjusting her bright red headscarf and beaded necklaces as if her appearance to them mattered.

Then, just as they were getting ready to leave, she grabbed for Kaya's hand with a strength that defied her size, sat bolt upright and urged Kaya back.

'Come, come here.'

'Everything OK?' Arno was back at her side in a heartbeat.

'I'm fine,' Kaya told him, registering the way he was studying her, as if he was afraid she might cower in fear of this poor patient, the way she had with Mikal yesterday on her way into the resort. She was already regretting that reaction, as if she could've helped it!

Arno prised the lady's hand gently from hers and she felt the sparks shoot up her arm at the gesture, his fingers brushing hers again. He cleared his throat and stepped away, dashing his head with the same hand. Did he feel some need to protect her now, because of the way she'd been yesterday, and today too, when she'd knocked the box of tests to the ground? That would be mortifying.

She was sure her cheeks were flaming red, but Mama Imka was still looking at her imploringly. Her eyes flickered to Arno. Then back to her.

'Let me read for you,' she croaked, pointing a finger her way. She gestured to another woman, younger—her daughter maybe—hovering in the doorway. 'Get me my shells.'

Arno busied himself with clearing away their equipment while Kaya was ordered to sit cross-legged on a woven mat on the mud floor. So, he wasn't going to save her from this, then?

Her heart was a lion, begging for release inside her chest. She had most definitely not come here to have her fortune told, but how was she supposed to get away now? The woman was already shuffling around from the makeshift bed and sliding to the floor opposite her, her skirts billowing around her.

A jar of what looked like seashells, bones, shiny stones and sticks was promptly opened and spilled in front of her. Mama Imka seemed to study the array of items for what felt like an eternity, frowning and chanting something under her breath, garnering some kind of message, she supposed.

'My dear, you have been through some hardships…' she started huskily. 'I see your past through a veil of tears, but your future is…'

She tailed off thoughtfully, glancing up at Arno conspicuously. Kaya's heart leapt to her throat. Why was she so nervous when she didn't even believe in all this stuff? *Everyone* had cried at some point in their past. OK, so maybe she'd shed a few more tears than most while she was putting the pieces of her life back together but, still, that was a pretty generic statement, taken from a bunch of shells, no less!

Arno stood somewhat awkwardly behind her, as if he too wished this would be over. Thankfully he left the hut, distracted by one of the children, before he could hear what the woman said next, because what Mama Imka went on to tell Kaya about life, and even potential *love* made her heart stop altogether, then slam like a bullet against her ribs.

She'd stew on these words in secret for the next two weeks.

CHAPTER FIVE

ON THE ROOF of the Jeep, Arno swigged from his coffee flask and studied the mountains across the reserve. This new birth of a day in all of its colourful motion was something he wished he could transfer to a canvas…but his mother was the painter, not him.

He sighed at the grass. He'd have to go home today, after his rounds. Dad had called yesterday, which sent the usual icy blast through his bones—they had never been close. Not since that night when they lost the baby and he told him, his only son, that he should've been there to protect Mama.

Going home was awkward to say the least. Arno still didn't enjoy the thought that he might see that blame in his father's eyes again one day…or in Mama's eyes. He could barely talk to Mama in case she confirmed she too blamed him for the miscarriage. Instead he did nice things when they asked him to, and made his polite exit soon after.

This time Dad had asked if he could come and oversee the removal of an old piece of furniture someone was coming to buy from the villa. He was heading overseas for a wine convention—and secretly didn't trust his wife not to sell the antique sideboard off cheap.

'No Tande this morning?'

A voice behind him made him start and he swung his legs over the side of the Jeep to address Kaya, walking towards him, a vision in the half-light. She was clutching a book to her chest.

'She doesn't get to come past the fence to the staff buildings…and good morning,' he said, taking in the sleepy yawn she failed to hide behind her hand, the loose cotton trousers with the zebra patterns on the sides that she might or might not have slept in. To his chagrin, he had thought a little too much about what Kaya might sleep in lately.

They hadn't really spoken much since that first day in the village, over two weeks ago now, not on a personal level anyway. But he'd found himself watching her, how poised she was, how hard-working and determined. She stood out in the group. She wasn't the chattiest, or the most social, so every time she laughed it was like a light coming on, and he was drawn to her undeniably, a bee to a honey tree. He'd been reminding himself it would do him no good to actually get her alone, or ask her what he wanted to ask—what had Mama Imka said?

'You're up early,' he said, motioning her over and pulling a tin cup from his backpack. 'Coffee?'

'You read my mind,' she said, placing her book on the roof and taking the cup of hot black liquid gratefully. She breathed a happy sigh over the rim. 'I thought I'd find a spot to read before breakfast. Then I saw you here, looking at the sky.'

'Another masterpiece, isn't it?' He gestured upwards with his cup and studied the angles of her face as she gazed in wonder at the screaming pink, now blazing a trail through the purple, and the mountain range beyond.

He was itching to ask her now. What did Mama Imka say? It shouldn't bother him so much, but she'd looked so shocked at the time, and he knew from experience that Mama Imka had hit a few nails on the head in the past, despite his scepticism in general.

Kaya had clammed up right after, spoken only about the garden and what she'd need to plant before the rains came—usually they arrived just a few weeks from now. The mystery made her ever more intriguing. He got the distinct impression she'd been told something she deemed to be life-changing, if indeed *she* even believed it.

'So, how are you doing?' he asked her now, as she sipped from her coffee cup on the ground below. She frowned as the cry of a rooster broke the silence and a passing zebra gave a dog-like bark in response.

'This is something I'm still getting used to,' she admitted, gesturing to the zebra now peering through the window to the mess hall, where breakfast would soon be served. There was a herd on the property, protected from the rest of the reserve and the hunters in it, like Tande.

'All these animals roaming freely. I mean, not too freely, I do feel quite safe here at the resort. And out there too, thanks to you.' She glanced at him quickly, then looked away too fast, and he caught something in her eyes that spoke loudly of what was clearly a mutual appreciation of the other. He cleared his throat, felt his hand dash his head of its own accord.

'I'm happy to hear that. I was hoping we could go check out the plot for the garden at some point. Maybe today? My guy in Cape Town has some timber up for grabs, he just needs to know how much to bring over.'

'I'm scheduled to be out in the mobile clinic till four,' she said quickly. 'With you…and some of the others.'

He nodded, noting her chewing her lip. Of course he knew the schedule. Didn't she want to be alone with him at all? He was not imagining this tension; he could feel it rising up between them like a hissing cobra. It wasn't as if he were suggesting a date though.

'We can go after,' he found himself saying. 'I know all the antigen tests came back negative but I need to check up on Mama Imka anyway.'

Kaya took a deep breath and closed her eyes, gripping her coffee cup tightly. 'Mama…right.'

'She got to you, huh?' He couldn't help it now. Her face after leaving that hut had said it all, but it wasn't as if he'd believed Mama Imka's predictions last time he'd let her read for *him*. When she'd said he had a big life ahead of him, and that a great love would bloom with the sunflowers.

There weren't any sunflowers growing anywhere in these parts, not that he knew of, and the thought of a big love coming his way was like expecting a spacecraft to land on the property—never going to happen. He hadn't so much as been on a date since Bea. Mostly because he cut them all off when they started asking if they could visit the winery. They were all only in it for the winery.

Or maybe he just didn't want to invite the kind of heartache that had knotted him up when he'd finally told Bea about how they'd lost his brother, and she'd gone on to ditch him not long after.

Kaya still hadn't spoken. When she realised

he was watching her she laughed to herself, shrugged and leaned back against the door of the Jeep, right by his legs. 'I don't know. I shouldn't have let her get to me, it's just that she was very…*specific* about some things and I'm still not sure what to think.'

'I wouldn't worry. I heard her say she saw your past through a veil of tears and people like you don't have time for tears.'

Kaya studied his boots a moment, then looked back up to the sky. 'People like me?'

'You've been so busy, becoming a qualified doctor, living your full fun life in a privileged first-world society…'

'Busy, privileged people can suffer hardships too, you know,' she bit back haughtily.

Damn, that clearly hadn't come out how he'd intended. He dropped to the floor with a dusty thud, went to refill her cup but she put a hand over it.

He shoved his flask into his backpack. 'I know that. I've been through my share of it too. I just meant…well.' He paused, rubbed his chin. What had he meant exactly? He'd been fishing for information on her and dug himself into a hole by insulting her instead.

'Sorry,' he offered. 'Maybe I was just curious. She gave my father a reading once, a long time ago. Me too, about a year ago, just after she fell sick.'

'What did she say?' Kaya's dark stare was flecked with the amber of the sunrise as she studied him. His thoughts whirled around in the depths of her eyes.

Mama Imka had seen the fire coming. She'd warned his father. He thought for one split second about telling Kaya this and didn't. Because then he'd have to tell her how he was out drinking instead of watching his mother when the fire broke out, how the three guys in the restaurant lost their lives; it was all too bleak for such a beautiful morning, and woman. And anyway, he was her mentor; he was supposed to be someone she could trust.

'You tell me yours, and I'll tell you mine,' he said instead, stepping closer on impulse and reaching out to brush a mosquito away from her arm.

Kaya stepped backwards immediately as if he'd drawn a gun on her, crossing her arms around herself.

'I can't...' she mumbled, eyeing him warily, then shaking her head. 'Sorry, it's not you, it's...'

'What's wrong?' he said now, concerned. 'I've noticed you're a little...tetchy when people get too close to you, even by accident.'

Kaya bristled and looked at him sideways before squaring her shoulders. 'Sorry.'

'Don't apologise,' he said, surprised at the softness in his own voice. There was nothing like a vulnerable woman to propel him into protector mode. Something about making up for what he did to Mama, he supposed. Dad had told him clearly before he left, just days before the fire: 'You need to look after your mama, son,' and he'd chosen to go out with his friends instead.

'Did something happen to you?' He frowned at her. He had to know.

'I'm totally fine.' Kaya's words were clipped, and she didn't meet his eyes. Then, before he could utter another word, she made an excuse to go back to her room.

Arno kicked himself. He'd gone too far.

He snatched up the book she'd left behind and put it on the back seat. She was harder to read than the Dutch text on the jacket. He'd have to return it later. Something told him he might get his marching orders if he followed her to her room and, besides, he'd been about to invite in questions he wouldn't know quite how to answer himself.

The village demanding their attention today was once again echoing with the sound of children laughing and playing. This time they were on a break from classes at the little school they'd parked Betsy, the mobile clinic, outside.

'They're so adorable and cheerful,' Kaya observed aloud to Arno, before she could think. She still felt pretty bad for scuttling off this morning mid-conversation, but her reflexes simply would not be retrained as easily as she hoped they might be.

'When you don't know what you're missing, I guess there's not much to be sad about,' he replied, opening a drawer and pulling out a stethoscope, then turning to the young woman who'd taken a seat, who was complaining of a sore throat.

Kaya worried she'd scared him off for good now. All he'd done was try to wave off a bug and she'd reacted as though he'd been about to assault her. Then, when he'd pretty much given her the opportunity to admit that yes, something terrible did happen to her once, and get it all out in the open—at least, with her mentor—she'd brushed him off instead. He probably thought she was cold as ice. Or frigid, as Pieter had said. But he wasn't Pieter. And enough time had passed since all that—she should have just said *something*.

It wasn't even that she didn't trust him. Look at the man, she thought, sneaking a quick glance at him in action, his muscles struggling to escape the short sleeves of his T-shirt as he monitored a woman's heartbeat, a look of consternation on his face that always made her wonder what selfless thought was running around in his head.

He'd been nothing but a muse, a teacher, and a… OK, yes, a gentleman tough to look away from. To her and everyone here over the last couple of weeks. So much so that she'd tried to keep her distance. Crushing on him was not a good idea, and would surely go nowhere for multiple reasons, but on top of all that, Mama Imka's cryptic words wouldn't leave her head:

'Pay attention, dear. If you see a snake as nothing but poison, poison is all it will be. You can learn from snakes, you see. They show us how you don't have to always move quickly. You can still get where you want to be, by crawling.'

There had been more, of course, a lot more from Mama Imka, about how a big love was waiting for her when she shed her old skin; something transformative with the power to change, not just her own circumstances, but others' too. Maybe she'd just been caught up in the moment but, through the cryptic mysticism that she'd been certain was all rubbish, Arno's snake tattoo refused to stop staring her in the face. It had taken on new meaning since then. Was it some kind of harbinger of transformation?

She kept telling herself she didn't believe in all that. That she was just projecting some hokum onto the first thing that seemed to reflect the woman's words. But still. It was difficult to look Arno in the eye without wanting to either run from him, or ask him what Mama Imka had said to *him*, *and* his father. He had kind of stared through her this morning when she'd asked, as if he was conjuring up something best left buried, which had set the alarm bells off in her head. Had something Mama Imka said to him, something *bad*, actually come true?

'Pass the iodine,' he was saying now, and when her fingers brushed his on the bottle between their chairs, she caught his eye and held it. Her heart revved as her hand seemed to linger next to his for longer than was probably necessary, all of its own accord, and she caught the hint of a smile on his mouth before they both turned back to their patients. Her pulse was a lump in her throat.

Maybe he didn't think she was an ice queen…

Across the mobile unit, Kimberley winked at her and Kaya rolled her eyes. She couldn't help the small smile that hovered on her lips a second though, before she bit it back.

She was assisting Arno, Kimberley and two other volunteers in seeing to the line of people that had formed as soon as the mobile clinic had pulled up. Arno had followed behind in his trusted Jeep. An hour in and they'd already diagnosed three respiratory conditions, bandaged several minor wounds, mainly to children's legs, knees and feet, and referred two cases of tuberculosis, which they'd done the same antigen tests for at the start of the week.

The Lindiwe Health Foundation's services were pivotal in maintaining the health of these small communities. What Arno had started was a miracle for these people, but what exactly, she wondered, had made him venture this far away from his family's wine business?

While she focused on her own patients at the next set-up station in the mobile unit, she couldn't help the way her eyes wandered to Arno. Every now and then she'd catch him looking at her too, as if he was trying to decode her or something, which sent her heart into a wild flurry of panic, excitement and adrenaline.

When he pulled her aside afterwards, and asked if she still wanted to go check on their garden plot, he looked as if he actively expected her to say no, which suddenly made her want to do the opposite.

'Why not?' she told him, and he raised his eyebrows, as if to ask if she was sure.

'Let's go,' she said, wondering exactly what was coming over her as she started towards the Jeep.

CHAPTER SIX

ARNO WATCHED AS Kaya used all her might to push the six-foot post into the hole in the ground. 'It's a little tight in this patch,' she said, heaving another breath. 'The ground is a bit too rocky.'

'Want some help?' He paused, wiping the sweat from his brow from the other end of the garden, where he'd just driven in another pole of his own in what would mark the end of the garden and the trellises for whatever vegetables Kaya wanted to plant.

'I'm fine,' she responded.

'Of course, you're fine,' he muttered under his breath, wondering when she'd admit she needed help. That pole of hers wouldn't last the night if they left it like that.

The afternoon sun was still beating down, even at five p.m. There were hints in the clouds that the sunset would be stunning, but he had to watch the time if he was still going to drop Kaya back, and then make it out to the estate to help Mama and her buyer with the sideboard.

'We could plant potatoes here,' Kaya was saying to a group of four young kids who'd gathered around her in curiosity. She'd abandoned her pole on the floor for now, and they seemed to be excited to dig in with their little shovels to help make the hole for it deeper.

Arno watched her crouch with her own little shovel, and explain about spinach, and Swiss chard, easy root plants like carrots, radishes and beetroot. She seemed to know as much about broccoli, cabbage, cauliflower, and kale as she did about anything they'd discussed in the mobile medical unit this morning. He couldn't help smiling when he overheard the kids ask if she'd brought them any candy, and got a firm no in response.

Mapping out the entire plot for the vegetable garden hadn't exactly been his plan but when the villagers got excited about something, it was all hands on deck. He had, however, told the gang of three local men waiting on the sidelines that Kaya wanted to do as much herself as possible.

It wouldn't do to feed whatever fear Kaya seemed to have of people she didn't know getting too close. She hadn't said as much, but it was obvious something had happened to her back home that she didn't want to talk about. Luckily she seemed fine with their patients. It was just men that put her on edge, he reminded himself; him included, sometimes. Maybe not as much now as when she'd first arrived.

Arno felt his brow crease and he looked away as he caught her eye. It was none of his business…just as whatever Mama Imka had said to her the other week was none of his business, even though having to keep his distance was somehow making him want to get even closer to his new recruit. He cared about what might have happened to her, he realised, even though he barely knew her. She seemed to carry as many mysteries with her as his friends liked to say *he* did.

Intriguing.

'Kaya!'

Pausing with his spade, he turned to where Mama Imka was waving at her from behind the pigpen across the dirt patch, simultaneously swiping away the flies. They'd given her a checkup before moving on to the garden project, so he wondered what she could want with Kaya as the woman proceeded to walk towards her, lifting her skirts as she strode purposefully her way.

'Shouldn't you be resting?' he called to the old lady, but she waved him away, mumbling something about resting when she was dead.

He swiped his hands on his trousers, and set to work with the measuring tape, trying not to look as if he were earwigging on what the women might now be discussing.

Five feet by five feet would be adequate space for a couple of stacked beehives, which Kaya had insisted they should also source from somewhere, he mused, turning his ear to them but failing to hear a thing over the snorting of a nearby pig. As yet he didn't know who he'd source beehives from, but it was a good idea for a bonus community project...

'Snake!'

What? The word had him turning to Mama Imka again, only to find Kaya was covering her face with her hands, despite the dirt.

'Snake,' Mama Imka stated, this time gesturing to his arm from across the way.

'This?' he mouthed, rubbing a hand over his tattoo and leaving a muddy streak across the scales. 'What about it?'

'Nothing,' Kaya said quickly, ushering the woman away. He heard her say she really had to be getting things done here before sunset and when he wandered over, he was finally allowed to help her...and her face was still bright, flushed with embarrassment.

Together they heaved the post up and kicked the soil back around it, holding it between them like a third person while the kids helped shovel the rest of the dirt around the base, excited to be able to lend a hand.

Inches from her face, Arno could've sworn she was avoiding his eyes. Behind Kaya, Mama Imka was standing with the guys on the sidelines, eyeing him over her can of iced tea, prodding her biceps where his tattoo was on his.

'What was all that about?' he asked, amused.

'I think she just likes your tattoo,' Kaya said, and he studied the streaks of dirt across her cheeks, resisting the urge to wipe some away.

'I hope she's not planning on getting one at her age,' he followed, and she huffed a laugh he could tell didn't come from her heart.

'Who knows?'

Just then, a loud noise from beyond the fence, followed by a shrill scream, made them both start and the kids abandon their positions at the base of their pole. Luckily it was now firmly in the ground, because what Arno saw next, raging around the corner and almost flattening the last hut in the row of humble homes, had both him and Kaya staggering backwards and into each other in shock.

'Is that Alma?' Kaya couldn't believe her eyes. The rescue elephant she'd seen briefly during her last visit here was rearing into their garden plot with the ferocity of a speeding train. Thick chains around her tree-trunk-like back legs had come loose from whatever she'd been tied to, and a poor guy in jeans and a flimsy shirt was being dragged behind her, screaming for mercy.

'We have to help him!' Kaya was about to lunge forwards, anything to help this poor man, who was covered in blood already. 'He's hooked onto her somehow…we have to get him loose!'

Arno stood like an impenetrable wall in front of her, blocking her path, holding a hand up to stop anyone else from moving. His hand went to his belt, where he usually kept a gun and a tranquilliser dart, but he cursed to himself. He'd left it in the Jeep. No one had expected…this.

'Everyone stay where you are,' he instructed, his voice low and laced with caution that sent her pulse to her throat.

Snapping out of it, Kaya went to run the other way towards the Jeep. They needed medical supplies, fast, but Arno gripped her elbow, fast as lightning, just as the elephant trumpeted so loudly a flock of birds took off into the sky. Then, to her horror, it turned towards her, ready to charge. Arno leapt in front of her again, and she clutched his arm from behind, peeking out, half expecting a full herd to appear in a stampede.

Mama Imka let out a cry and a plea to the elephant to stop. She was clutching the hands of two young children who'd run up to her for comfort. The rest of the village had gathered now, shouting at full volume, waving their arms, making themselves bigger than the elephant.

Releasing her fingers from their steel grip around Arno's snake-tattooed biceps, Kaya joined in, flapping her arms in the air, yelling *shoo, shoo*, like they were, as if it were a mouse! The elephant staggered to the left, straight into the pole Arno had just pushed into the ground, and completely flattened it.

The elephant's poor victim was losing a lot of blood, mostly from his leg. A groan escaped his lips as he narrowly avoided being crushed by the pole. Kaya could see now he was hooked to the elephant by a chain around his own wrist. There was no way his arm wasn't broken too.

'I need you to help me,' Arno said to her.

Kaya was focused on the blood. The shock of what she was witnessing was only now registering—a wild animal gone truly rogue, stomping her disagreements out wherever she pleased, regardless of which humans here had shown her kindness or mercy up till now. No animals were really tame, none of them, she thought, not even Tande.

'Kaya.' Arno took her shoulders, and she didn't reel backwards. Rather, she felt grounded, hoisted back down to earth in one split second by his eyes. The groans of the man on the ground tore at her heart, especially since they couldn't reach him yet, but he was alive, and conscious.

'She's slowing down, she knows she's cornered,' Arno told her as the villagers closed in, still holding their arms high, fearlessly. 'We'll go in, together, do what I do,' he said, eyes darting past her to the Jeep. 'We need to get him to the vehicle. It's the safest place. We need to put an object between us...'

'OK,' she heard herself say, looking around for something and spotting the pole at the same time. She followed his lead, picked up the other end of the fallen pole, and together they walked as one giant barrier slowly towards Alma.

'That's it, slowly, you got this,' he encouraged her as they heaved the pole up together. It was the strangest, not to mention heaviest object she'd ever approached an emergency scene with, but an otherworldly strength seemed to possess her as they took slow but purposeful strides as one, towards the creature and her unfortunate victim.

As if sensing she was well and truly cornered now, Alma lowered to her fat, wrinkly knees in front of them. With one final trumpet she swept the floor with her trunk, and blew a shower of sand up around them, followed by a cascade of mud from a puddle on the ground, where a bucket had been spilled. Both Kaya and Arno were covered instantly.

A man appeared then with a tranquilliser dart…too little, too late, Kaya thought, struggling to hold the pole, as hot, wet mud trickled down her forehead into her eyes.

'Don't shoot!' Arno was adamant, blinking mud from his own eyes. 'She's fine, this man is not her keeper, he was standing in, she must have just got spooked,' he explained, inching closer, and motioning for her to lower the pole. It hit the dirt with a thud and she finally ran for the Jeep, swiping at her face.

Crouching with the medical-aid kit, she helped Arno roll the man onto his back. He was conscious, but badly wounded. 'How far was he dragged?' she asked incredulously as the elephant seemed to sigh close by and put her head to the ground.

'Not so far, but she may have stood on his leg,' Arno observed, frowning at the flesh wound, the fragments of bone emerging from below his left knee. 'This is beyond us, Kaya,' he said grimly. 'He'll need to be airlifted out of here.'

He readied a tourniquet and she bandaged it as best she could while he radioed for help. A crowd of villagers had gathered around the elephant now. One bearded old man was bravely trying to get her up, to lead her away, while Kaya and

Arno helped their survivor to the Jeep. The air ambulance would fly in from Cape Town, and as the seconds ticked past their patient groaned and clutched her hand, and insisted it wasn't the elephant's fault.

'He'll be OK,' Arno assured her, placing a hand on her arm gently. 'Will *you*?'

'I already am,' she said, searching his warm eyes. A moment passed…something realigned inside her like a shift between tectonic plates. Then Arno removed his hand, way too quickly, as if she were lava that might burn him.

Her fault, of course.

Kaya swallowed the annoyance at the way she'd inadvertently shunned him and, worse, made him think she was some little weak thing with issues, when clearly she'd just found the strength, somehow, to face off an elephant. All she'd felt at that touch was warmth, and a strange kind of certainty she wasn't used to: that not every man had the potential to hurt her. Some only had her best interests at heart.

Several women and children were crying, and, through the whirlwind of activity, Kaya noticed how Arno was nothing short of a hero, comforting their patient with her, consoling the poor man's wife when she arrived on the scene, ensuring that no harm would come to the spooked elephant.

Maybe she should've just told him what had happened to her back in Amsterdam, when she'd had the chance this morning. He wasn't the kind of man to dismiss her as an unsuitable employee because of it. He was a good person. The fact that something deep in her gut was thawing and learning to thrive again—albeit slowly—was giving her a spring to her step she'd thought she'd never have again, and he was partly the cause.

It hit her then, as the helicopter flew into view, that she hadn't told him anything because it wasn't just her professionalism she was afraid he might question. What Arno thought about *her* was starting to matter.

Her unfortunate crush was growing bigger by the minute, and that would have to be nipped in the bud. He was quite a few years older than her, she reminded herself, watching him lift his muddy shirt up over his head, revealing a body so muscled and toned she had to do a double take, then force her eyes away from his rippling abs. Sadly, he replaced his shirt with another from the Jeep, and went to address the paramedics.

They came from different worlds, she thought, packing up the equipment, rinsing her hands off with bottled water, glancing his way, catching him catching *her* watching him—again.

This is ridiculous.

He was not some saviour sent to sweep her up and fix her. And even if he *was* attracted to her too, she was no good at relationships, or even hook-ups. Her instinctive reactions to being touched were so embarrassing she hadn't even *dared* to go on one date since Pieter had put a worse taste in her mouth than her perpetrator ever had, going behind her back with someone else—someone she knew, no less. What if he realised her ability to be intimate—in that way—was broken, and left her…?

Climbing back into the Jeep, her thoughts a mile a minute, Kaya realised with dismay that the garden plot would need to be entirely redone, and that *she* had no clean clothes to change into at all. She was absolutely caked head to toe in mud, and it was at least an hour's drive back to Thabisa.

CHAPTER SEVEN

ARNO SWIPED THE mud from his face as he drove back to the main road. The events of the last hour had put him on an adrenaline high, but now he was coming back down to earth and he saw only one option. He had no time to take Kaya to Thabisa before heading back to the estate to help his mama. She would have to come with him.

When he asked if she minded, she looked horrified. 'Like *this*?' She gestured to her filthy clothes and pulled the visor down, swiping another streak from her neck in the mirror. He couldn't help smiling. She looked kind of adorable, even now that she was covered in mud.

He should offer to hurry up in the house while she stayed in the Jeep, but no…that would definitely not be the right thing to do, he mused. She was his responsibility. She'd just risked her life in the face of an angry elephant, and he was doubting whether to let her use his mother's bathroom?

What is wrong with you, Arno?

'You can take a quick shower while I help Mama with the sideboard,' he told her, before he could even think. What would be the harm in that anyway? She wouldn't even see the blackened walls, or spend longer than three minutes with his mother, there would be no time for her to find out what an irresponsible son he really was… They'd be in and out, back on the road before it got dark.

Kaya's eyes grew wide as he swept the dirty Jeep through the gates of the Nkosi Valley Wine Estate. Nestled in the picturesque Blaauwklippen Valley, it was a highlight of Stellenbosch, even now, even though several areas hadn't ever been rebuilt after the fire.

'It's so beautiful,' Kaya enthused, taking in the sweeping rows of vines as far as the eye could see, framed by the mountains in the late afternoon sun. The yellow stone villa up ahead put a lump in his throat, but he forced indifference about bringing her here. She wasn't to know he hadn't let anyone here in a long time, for the one selfish reason that they might learn something awful about him as Bea had.

'Our ancestors had the vineyards planted on the slopes of the Helderberg Mountain, where the breeze comes in over the ocean,' he found himself saying, slowing down so she could take in the views. This would be the one time she'd see it, he supposed. 'The breeze helps add the freshness to the wines,' he continued, surprised at the tour-guide tone he was taking; it was just that she looked so enchanted.

'We used to have a cellar door, so people on tours would stop in and try the wines, have a meal at the restaurant…'

'There's a restaurant here? Ooh, what kind of food?'

Arno bit his cheek. 'Well, it hasn't been open for twenty years now.'

'Why not?'

Arno paused, pulling the Jeep to a stop. Here they came: the questions. Thankfully Mama was already sweeping down the front steps, dressed in her orange kaftan, covered in paint splotches as usual. She lunged for a hug the second he stepped onto the gravel.

'So wonderful to see you, my baby,' she swooned, pressing a palm to his cheek, making Kaya raise her eyebrows at him on the other side of the Jeep. 'I saw you from the studio. It's good of you to come help. You know your father doesn't trust me not to give that old sideboard away for less than it's worth. He's probably right, it's just in the way…'

As she chattered on about the chore he was here to do, he found himself noticing a few more lines around Mama's eyes, a couple of new wrinkles around her mouth. A paintbrush protruded through her mass of thick, greying hair, where she'd stuck it behind her ear.

'You have more paint on you than we do mud,' he announced, clearing his throat, looking around for his father, even though he knew he wasn't there. He hated how being here made the guilt flare up ten thousand-fold, and that he couldn't seem to talk to Mama at all about it in case it *was* justified.

Mama only then seemed to realise they were filthy dirty. 'Goodness, you're right, what happened to you two?'

'We had a little brush with an elephant,' Kaya told her, holding out her hand. 'I'm Kaya.'

Arno winced. 'Sorry, sorry, Kaya, the inimitable Mama Annika Nkosi.' How embarrassing that he hadn't introduced her first; it wasn't as if he ever brought people home though, he was out of practice. He watched the women shake hands, the way Mama looked at her with her own special warmth, feeling the knot in his stomach tighten.

'I said she could take a quick shower, if that's OK?'

'Of course, go right ahead,' Mama said, ushering them both up the stairs to the veranda, and into the hallway. Kaya's eyes went to the family photos on the walls that stretched all the way up the staircase. Generations of Nkosis, who'd made the winery what it was.

'I'm making some tea, you'll have some first,' she announced, motioning them through to the kitchen.

'Oh, we don't have much time, we're just going to wait for your man, he's due any minute, right?' Arno went to usher Kaya towards the bathroom instead. But she was already staring at the blackened walls around the barricaded kitchen door, which had once led into their beautiful restaurant.

They'd had the bedroom where his mother had been that night completely renovated. Even the restaurant walls had been reconstructed. On the outside it was good as new, but inside… His mother had insisted they leave the fire-licked bricks on show around the barricades to remind them to stay humble, to be aware that life could change in a heartbeat, and to always be grateful. She said she saw it like a piece of art.

'What's that?' Kaya said, wrinkling her nose quizzically at the bricks before he could even get her back to the door. 'Did there used to be a fireplace there?'

'That's where the restaurant was,' his mother said, pondering the wall with her now, twiddling a strand of her long, grey hair around the paintbrush behind her ear.

'Oh, right, Arno said it hasn't been open for a while?'

Arno felt his heart change gears in his chest. 'We'll take our tea to go, Mama. The bathroom is through there.' He pointed to the arched alcove across the terracotta floor, resisting the urge to put a hand to Kaya's mud-splattered back and guide her there even faster. 'Towels are in the cupboard; use anything you like.'

She shot him a look of mild annoyance mixed with confusion, but he plastered a smile to his face, just as his mother offered to get her some clean clothes.

'I can change when we get back,' Kaya started, embarrassed.

'Nonsense, you can't get back into dirty clothes, it's no trouble.'

Kaya nodded, seemingly unsure what to think, just as he was.

'She seems nice. One of your volunteers?' Mama said, turning to him with a choice of teas when Kaya was safely in the terracotta-tiled bathroom.

'She is,' he replied, picking out a rosehip tea he thought Kaya would like, and a mint one for himself, then letting himself sink into a wooden chair at the dining table. He fiddled with the wax on a melted candle, letting his eyes wander back to the kitchen wall. Sometimes he thought about painting over it, or having new bricks installed over the hotch-potch of wooden planks across the old doorway, so he wouldn't have to look at it. But that would be selfish. Mama had the right to remember things how she wanted.

He twitched again, remembering the plaque he'd designed but still hadn't had made. *Remembering Baby Kung.* That was what it said. He wanted it to go on this very wall…one day. He'd never got round to it, in case it brought back all the hurt. For all of them.

'Should we move the sideboard outside so your man can collect it easier when he gets here?' he said now, standing up before any more uncomfortable memories could wriggle back into his brain.

'Sure, but first let me grab some clothes. Your Kaya girl has a wicked figure, I have the perfect thing I want her to try on.'

'Mama, you really don't have to…'

His protest fell on deaf ears. His mother was already halfway out of the door.

When Kaya emerged fresh and clean from the bathroom, Arno and his mother were outside. Through the wide arched windows overlooking the sweeping vineyards and majestic mountains, she spotted Arno talking with a tall man, who

seemed to be hosing down the Jeep. Mama Annika was on the phone.

Kaya couldn't resist a sneaky look around the
lower level of the house. She'd never been to a
winery before. This was in fact the hugest house
she'd ever stepped foot in, though the charred-
looking walls were a little strange. She wandered
over, stroked a finger over the bricks, only to find
soot on her fingertips. There must have been a
fire at some point. Was *that* why they closed the
restaurant? Arno seemed kind of…what was the
word he'd used with her…*tetchy* about something, now that they were here.

She was still frowning at her fingertips when
Arno strode back in, looking more than a little
disgruntled. 'He can't come and get the sideboard
till the morning now,' he grumbled as she wiped
her hands quickly behind her back. 'Something
about getting side-tracked by…'

He tailed off when he saw what she was wearing. Mama Annika had left her something pretty
unexpected outside the bathroom door. Kaya literally saw his eyes wander from the scooped
neckline of the chic olive-green dress, to the
nipped in waist, right down to the hem just above
her knees, and back up again to her still-damp
hair.

Self-consciousness sent her questions about
the closed-off restaurant rushing from her brain

in a poof. She flushed in his stare. Usually, under this much scrutiny from a man, she'd want to run a mile, yet his eagle-like attention sent a shower of sparks right through her.

'You look…different,' he said, as if trying to fathom how there was someone mildly attractive under the mud, and the uniform tees she usually wore in his presence. She bit back a smile.

'Different, good?' she dared, surprising herself. Was she *flirting*?

He cleared his throat, picked up a flowery teacup quickly from the table and handed it over. 'Before it gets cold,' he said, just as Mama Annika walked back in and gave a rather more enthusiastic reaction.

'Oh, my sweet child, how good does that look on you?' she cried, practically dancing over and forcing her to take a spin on the spot. Her tea almost went flying. 'I had a feeling it would, I'm far too big for it these days. You keep it, it suits you, doesn't it, Arno? Doesn't she look amazing?'

Arno bobbed his head and mumbled his agreement, looking as if he wanted to run away. His mother seemed oblivious to her son's embarrassment. 'Now, I suppose Arno told you the sideboard can't be collected till seven a.m. tomorrow? You might as well stay for dinner, seeing as you're here now.' She beamed at her, clapped her hands together. 'Stay the night?'

Arno sprang from the chair. 'No, no, Mama, we really have to be going…'

'And drive all the way back here for me, first thing in the morning?' she tutted. 'Don't be ridiculous. I'll have the guest rooms made up, you can drive back right after he collects the sideboard in the morning, what's the harm? You can show Kaya the vines…and the tasting room, and the memorial.'

Memorial?

Mama Annika pottered over to the fridge, spouting delicious local food items she would prepare for them, and Kaya was amused at the way Arno looked completely mortified for a moment. It was almost as if he thought this was the biggest inconvenience on earth. It really wasn't that much of a big deal, and she told him so, taking a seat at the rustic farmhouse table with her tea. It seemed as if his mother liked having him around, and she'd never spent the night on a vineyard before.

He didn't seem keen on her being here with him though. He probably thought this whole thing was turning into something completely unprofessional and weird. He simply couldn't say no to his mother; that was the only reason they were both still here.

But she hadn't been made to feel quite this sexy in a long time, nor confused about her feelings for someone. It was all new and suddenly quite exciting. Maybe she wasn't entirely broken, she thought as he sloped past her to take a shower, catching her eyes again and sending a flock of butterflies straight to her stomach. Maybe she'd just needed a real crush this whole time to bring her back to life. She'd taken Pieter's words to heart: 'frigid', 'cold'. She'd let them burn her, let them force an iron cage around her heart when she'd labelled herself undesirable and undeserving of love long before he ever did.

The shell was coming away, slowly, every second she found herself attracted to Arno. She was melting, she realised. This man was enforcing a kind of slow defrost and her crush was bringing her in from the cold.

But a crush was all it could be—Arno Nkosi was entirely off limits. He might as well wear a giant sign reading 'Do Not Touch'.

Kaya sighed, picturing the way the water must be sliding down his body in the shower. Then she recalled how quickly he'd pulled away from her, when he'd asked if she was OK earlier. Right when she could have sworn they'd been having a moment.

She still hadn't explained to him why she'd shut down on him a few times already; why it was hard for her to let anyone physically close to her, particularly men. It wasn't as if she'd spoken about the effects of the assault to anyone, not after Pieter cheated. It was all too humiliating.

But at least if she told Arno *something* about the attack, he'd know it wasn't really *him* she was wary of. At least he'd know she didn't mean to insult his kindness.

The thought of having such a conversation sent chills through her bones, even in the warm kitchen.

CHAPTER EIGHT

ARNO'S PHONE RANG halfway through dinner—a contact at the hospital who found them after he'd told Thabisa they wouldn't be back. Their elephant survivor was doing fine post-surgery. He'd broken his leg and sprained a wrist but, other than shock, he'd been pretty lucky. Taking his seat again, Arno noticed his mother had moved away from the conversation he'd been trying to keep on the Lindiwe Health Foundation and Kaya's vegetable garden plans, and started asking Kaya about life in Holland.

'It's as you'd expect, pretty busy. I spent most of the time in the hospital with my work.'

'Don't people cycle everywhere? Is the cheese as good as they say?'

The questions kept coming, and while Arno was indeed intrigued to know more about her and her life, which she always seemed to keep close to her chest, he couldn't ignore that Kaya was clearly feeling less than comfortable in the spotlight.

Before long, he had her out on the veranda around the firepit, while his mother thankfully took a phone call from an old friend inside. The tension rose between them the second they were alone. He'd wondered if it would. Something seemed to have changed today and he didn't know if it was because of what happened in the village with the elephant, or because she was here…at his family home…in that dress…but he didn't quite know what to do with it.

'So, your mother mentioned a memorial somewhere?' she said now, pulling the woollen blanket he'd given her tighter around her shoulders. The moonlight played in her hair and danced across her cheekbones and he wondered what her lips would be like to kiss, even as his stomach clenched at her words. He tossed another chunk of wood onto the firepit. He'd been hoping she'd forgotten that.

'Is that, like, for a dog you had once? A cat? I know you love your animals.'

He huffed a laugh. 'It's not for any animals,' he said. 'Mama had it built for…some people who died.'

'Here?' Kaya pulled a face and glanced out at the vines, as if a ghost might suddenly pop up between the bunches of Sauvignon Blanc. He nodded, his heartbeat ratcheting up a notch.

'They didn't die in a fire, did they?' she said, frowning at him over the flames now. 'Arno, what happened here?'

Arno sank to his haunches prodding the flames again, as if he could get some tiny revenge on the element that had ruined the place; and would probably ruin what Kaya thought about him, too, if he told her everything. She'd seen the walls, heard about the restaurant, she'd put the pieces together.

Standing up, he beckoned her with him around the house, down the now-dark pathway between the vines. She looked a little nervous when he turned to check on her, and again he had to force himself not to reach for her hand. 'It's OK. Trust me,' he said.

'I do,' she replied, and the moonlight in her eyes as she searched his threw him off track for a moment. Was it the adrenaline, making him want to kiss her? The fact that he'd never brought anyone out here? The last thing he'd expected when they left Thabisa this morning was this. But here they were.

'What are you going to show me?' she asked, continuing on with him towards the barn where the barrels were stacked and the old bottles were gathering dust, and the new ones still lured the tourists *and* the locals in for tastings. He slid the giant door across, blinked with her into the blacked-out abyss, breathed the familiar smell of tannins and oak, and flipped the light switch.

Even without the restaurant, which used to be the unequivocal best restaurant around for miles, people still came to Nkosi Valley. Mostly these days, they just wanted to see the memorial.

'This is incredible!'

Kaya looped around the towering structure again, trying to soak in the entirety of the spectacle she was looking at. This was nothing short of a work of art. Framed photographs of three people stood out in the tree-like tower, surrounded by colourful trinkets that were all made from items related to wine. Bottles, screw tops, a halo made from corks...

'Did your mama make this?' she asked, studying the photos. Each one had a name under it, fashioned from yet more trinkets, coins and jewels. Marios, Anaya and Zen.

Arno, who'd said nothing up to now, walked up behind her and folded his arms slightly awkwardly and told her yes, it had all taken Mama Annika a year.

The memorial was at least eight feet high, stretching almost to the wooden beamed ceiling of the barn. Behind them, rows and rows of barrels, shelves stacked with wine right up to the rafters and a small circular bar with high stools around it told her this was the heart of the estate. Or used to be.

'There was a fire,' Arno said now, pressing his hands into his pockets. 'Twenty years ago. I was eighteen years old when it happened. These people worked for us.' He bobbed his head at the photos. 'They lost their lives that night.'

'I'm so sorry.' Kaya's heart had dropped to the pit of her stomach at the look on his face. 'That's how come the restaurant is closed…' she said.

'That's where the fire broke out. They mention reopening it every few years or so, but I think they're secretly afraid it would never be as good as it was. Restaurateurs are proud people, prouder of fixing people up than doctors are—that's what Mama said once.'

'Were you here when it happened?' she asked, resisting the urge to put a hand on his shoulder suddenly at his wry smile, realising she hadn't wanted to offer a man any form of comfort for anything in years; not till now, in this very moment.

'I wasn't home when it started,' he said tightly, avoiding her eyes. 'I should have been, but I wasn't.'

'Well, maybe you got lucky,' she offered, and he scowled darkly at the structure, scuffed up a fallen cork from the floor and strode past her to the bar.

'I should have been here. I was meant to get Mama up from her nap to eat. If I'd done that, then maybe we both would've smelled the fire next door sooner, before it spread.'

Kaya watched as he lifted a latch and stepped into the circular bar, closing it behind him.

'I got home to find it out of control. Mama somehow slept through it. I just managed to get her out. Marios, Anaya and Zen—the chef— were in the restaurant, trying to stop it spreading to the house; they were so dedicated to saving this place, they neglected to save themselves.'

'Arno… This is…' Kaya swallowed, trying to digest his words. What a tragedy! To think of what he, and all these people, must have gone through.

He reached for two wine glasses from the rack above him and she studied his movements, almost afraid to ask. But she had to.

'Where were you? That night.'

He sniffed. 'Out with friends. Drinking.'

She bit her cheeks and crossed to the bar, took a stool and watched him pour from a bottle. It wasn't wine. He hadn't drunk since he was eighteen, she remembered now. It must have been that night that put him off.

He pushed a glass towards her. 'Non-alcoholic,' he confirmed, resting an arm across the bar, putting the snake tattoo right in front of her face as he twirled his own glass and studied the pale yellow liquid inside. 'Nkosi Grape Elixir is one of our bestsellers.'

Kaya took a sip but she barely tasted it. His proximity and the severity of his words had left her in shock.

'I'm sure your family will want to reopen the restaurant one day. It has been twenty years,' she pressed.

Arno shrugged, chugging the grape juice back, then running his eyes over her mouth as she finally tasted it for herself. It was delicious, smooth, slightly tart…but she was more aware of how his eyes on her mouth had sent a little drummer boy right back into her chest.

'I can't help feeling responsible, you know,' he said, scanning her eyes now, as if he was looking for her to confirm that he might have been to blame.

'Why? You didn't start the fire,' she said.

'No, but, like I said, I might have been able to stop it. We lost the harvest that year, flames took out a whole pasture and the ash ruined the rest. The media were everywhere. I couldn't get away from their questions, especially after Mama lost…' He pulled back suddenly, swiped their glasses and turned his back to run them under the tap.

'Mama lost what?'

'Nothing,' he said quickly. 'I mean, every-thing, she lost everything. It felt like it anyway. Losing three staff members, seeing others in-jured… I guess that's what got me into medi-cine. I knew I had to help, do whatever I could, you know.'

'So that's how you started out with the foun-dation.'

'And I'll never go back.' He smirked then. 'You can't run a winery if you don't drink. You're not exactly a credible cheerleader for your stock when all you can rave about is the grape juice.'

Kaya didn't know what to say. What could she say?

'I'm so sorry you and your family went through all that, Arno,' she managed.

She didn't even know where she'd found the strength suddenly. Maybe it was hearing him share something so deeply personal, letting her see this remorseful, vulnerable side to him that she'd never seen before, but the words were coming out of her mouth before she could re-ally think.

'While we're sharing the things that might or might not still affect us, something pretty bad *did* happen to me, too,' she said. 'I brushed you

off when you asked before, because it's kind of...
well, I didn't want you to think me unprofessional, or unsuitable for this job.'

Arno pressed a hand over hers, on top of the
bar, sending a current up her entire arm. His
warmth and the protective gesture flooded her
senses, and as he went to pull his hand away
again, she caught it in her own, held onto him.
His eyes searched hers and she tried to pinpoint
his expression. Sadness, empathy, anger on her
behalf. It was all there, so clear it made her mind
go blank for a second.

'I knew it,' he said, looking down at their
hands. Kaya was suddenly glad the bar top was
between them, or else she might have gone one
step further and thrown her arms around him. He
wasn't to know but, to her, initiating a continued
touch like this was like leaping over a giant wall.
'What happened?' he asked her gently.

She took a deep breath. She hadn't spoken
about it to anyone who wasn't in her immediate
circle, let alone a man she barely knew. But Arno
was different; someone she could trust implicitly. He'd been through pain as great as hers, and
pain was a stronger bonding glue than anything.

'I was in a park in Amsterdam, late at night.
A man came at me out of nowhere,' she said, and
Arno's other hand came down over hers, clamping them together while she caught her breath.

'He threw me off my bike onto the ground, dragged me into the bushes. I thought he was going to kill me.' She swallowed, realising her hands had started to sweat and her voice was shaking. 'He tried to…he would have…he got into my underwear.'

'Kaya!' The rage on his face sent her pulse through the roof; he looked furious now, and she was struggling to maintain her composure.

'I managed to kick him off me,' she said. 'Some guys heard me shouting. They pulled up on their bikes and he got spooked and ran off. I never even saw his face. The police did nothing. They said there was nothing they could do.'

'It wasn't on camera?'

'There weren't any cameras in the park.'

His brow creased and he sucked in a breath through his nose and did not let go of her hands. They were silent for a moment. Then he finally lifted the latch and stepped out from the bar.

'That explains why you don't like to be touched,' he observed, stopping an inch from her shoes. Her hands were still hot from having his palms over them and strangely, she wanted him close again. She *wanted* his touch.

'Not usually,' she admitted, meeting his eyes again. She considered continuing, telling him what Pieter had said, how his words and actions had forced her further into her shell and left her with a fear of rejection so profound she'd never even considered dating again, till now.

Then again, Arno didn't need to know any of that. Pieter was the past, she was as much to blame for letting him get to her for so long, and this was…something different.

Arno stepped closer suddenly, as if testing her. He reached for both her hands, slowly and deliberately. 'Is this OK?' he said softly, turning her hands over in his as if they were precious, fragile items. Kaya felt another chunk of the glacier around her heart melt away.

'It's OK.' She gulped, thanking the heavens that he couldn't see into her brain. Suddenly, she'd never wanted a moment to last longer than this one, right now. It felt as if they were sharing something more than just the struggles they'd both encountered up till now. Her senses had never been so attuned to the movements of one person.

When he reached out to sweep a strand of hair from her forehead, the look in his eyes was so intense, so utterly surreal, it sent a jolt of fear through her like lightning. This was something big already. To her. It was something that could go very, very wrong, and potentially destroy her.

'We can't…' she muttered, pulling away quickly, leaving his hand in mid-air and turning to the barn door. 'I'm really tired…'

Within five minutes she'd shut herself in a guest room, where she lay awake for hours, wondering what on earth was happening to her.

As the weeks went past after that, Kaya did her best to maintain her professionalism around Arno, to tell her heart not to race in his presence. Just because they'd shared a few moments together, and he'd managed to crack a hole in the frosty cage she called her heart, it did not mean she could start obsessing over some potential fling.

This was a *temporary* position, a chance to feel alive, and useful and, OK, fine, maybe a little desirable every now and then after years of telling herself she could never feel that way again…but she was not here to put her heart in harm's way.

Arno was everything she didn't need to be all caught up in, and he was clearly still working through his own troubled past. It was so awful, what happened to those three people. He must think about it all the time.

Definitely better not to get any more personal, she told herself, about a thousand times.

However, the more she stayed away from Arno, the more he seemed to stay away from her, and before long, she barely had a thought left for the past. Confusion and frustration over her mounting attraction were occupying every neuron in her brain.

CHAPTER NINE

THE DAYS WERE flying by lately, things were so busy. From his set-up outside Betsy, the mobile clinic, Arno sneaked another glance at Kaya. She was looking particularly lovely today with her hair piled high on the top of her head, doing her kind, smiling thing for every single patient approaching her. But then, he thought she looked lovely every day, even in her blue shirts, as opposed to the olive-green dress Mama Annika had put her in that night.

She was a knockout.

He forced his eyes back to his patient's newly bandaged knee, right as Kaya caught him looking at her. Picturing her in and out of that dress had kept him up at night lately, as much as all the stuff they'd shared that night in the barn. He wished he didn't have to keep imagining her naked—she was not deserving of that, and she certainly wouldn't welcome it, maybe not from anyone, not after…what she'd been through.

She was walking over now, the afternoon sun in her hair. He pretended not to notice till she was literally standing behind his patient, in front of him.

'Sorry to interrupt, Arno, we're missing a box of leaflets for the presentation,' she said.

They were presenting together after this round at a rural primary school, part of his wider plan to have the foundation empower communities to act together with health, education and other social services like theirs. It wasn't like him to forget the handouts. Then again, he'd been pretty distracted lately, having Kaya around, knowing she knew what happened with the fire.

Did she know the rest?

It wouldn't be hard to find out about his dead baby brother. The media had lapped it up. All she'd have to do was search the Internet. She'd wonder why he didn't tell her that part.

'Arno?'

She was tapping her wrist now, and he realised his head was full of her, whether she was standing in front of him or not.

He dismissed his thankful patient, who hobbled away, grateful for the freshest bandage he'd had in a week. 'I'll go look in the back,' he said, annoyed with himself.

'I already looked,' she told him, stepping up into the vehicle behind him.

Alone in the mobile clinic, the walls closed in immediately. They didn't speak as they rifled through boxes, but the air was thick and the silence was loaded. Usually there would be other volunteers around, but Kimberley was sick with a stomach bug, and because of the presentation later, which Kaya had prepared for the school closest to this community, it had been the best thing for he and Kaya to kill two birds with one stone.

How could he deny his attraction to her? It was real, and affecting him daily, even if there was nothing he could do about it. She was no doubt several years his junior *and* she lived in the Netherlands, and she'd pulled away from him more times than he could count—not that he could blame her!

He was still kicking himself for the way he'd gone too far, reaching for her face like that, acting on the urge to be closer. Especially after what she'd told him about being assaulted—that was a stupid move. Besides, he didn't mess with volunteers. He just…didn't. Whatever their age, or background, or how unnervingly beautiful and captivating they were, it was just a bad idea, mixing business with pleasure…wasn't it?

Now he wasn't so sure.

Maybe he'd let Bea mess him up more than he'd thought. Bea hadn't been a volunteer, but she was an exceptional woman he'd poured his heart out to, who'd deemed him unworthy and disappeared. Not a great feeling.

Ever since that night around the memorial, they'd both kept their distance. Only the occasional eye contact and blush on her cheeks told him she was feeling the same as him…as if they'd hovered on some dangerous precipice together and didn't know what to do next.

'I don't see the leaflets. We must have left them at base,' he told her now, accidentally brushing her arm as he moved another box. 'Sorry,' he said, flustered at her proximity after all these weeks.

'Sorry for what?' she said, a frown darkening her face. He shrugged, held up his hands, and she cast her eyes to the ceiling. 'I'm not some precious little broken flower, you know, Arno. Just because I told you what I told you doesn't mean…' She huffed back her next words, mumbling to herself as she opened another box too roughly.

'Woah,' he said, catching her arm this time. 'What's going on?'

She blinked at him. 'I shouldn't have told you what I told you, that night in the barn.'

'Why not?'

She scowled into the box, scrubbed a hand across her head. 'You've hardly said one word

to me since. It's like, you're looking at me differently, and that's the last thing I wanted…'

'Kaya.' He stared at her, stunned. 'You haven't
spoken to me either,' he said. 'I thought I'd
messed up. I thought I'd crossed some line with
you I shouldn't have crossed. I was trying to be
respectful.'

Arno's head was spinning now.

'Well…' She chewed on her lip, hands on
hips, then blew out a sigh. 'I thought maybe
I'd crossed a line by telling you what happened
to me. It's not your burden to carry, you have
enough going on, all by yourself. I wasn't trying to overshadow what happened to your family and your friends in the fire.'

'I didn't think you were,' he said. 'It's not a
competition, who's been dealt the worst hand.
We were both just…being honest.'

Arno turned away before her eyes could probe
him any further. *He* hadn't been entirely honest, purposefully omitting the part about Mama
Annika being pregnant when the fire broke out.

Sure, he'd chickened out on telling Kaya the
whole truth, completely negated to mention what
a monumental error he'd *really* made, not being
home that night with Mama, but he couldn't bear
it if she started looking at *him* differently as Bea
had. Being able to trust people was everything
to Kaya.

'And for the record,' he added, feeling his fist clench at his side, 'I don't look at you any differently because of what you told me. Why the hell would I? If I'd known you when that happened to you, Kaya, I would've gone out with my rifle and knocked on every door in Amsterdam till I found who did that to you. And then…' He trailed off at the wide-eyed look of shock on her face, bit back the anger that was bubbling up on her behalf. 'You don't even want to know what I'd have done then.'

Kaya was still staring at him in disbelief, the pile of boxes and missing leaflets forgotten. 'My boyfriend never said *anything* like that,' she told him quietly.

Boyfriend?

Arno gritted his teeth. How had he failed to imagine she might be in a relationship? Why did that suddenly matter?

'Dr Nkosi? We need you out here!' The voice that broke into the mobile unit was laced with urgency. Before he could ask her anything about her boyfriend, he was racing with Kaya back out into the heat.

Kaya squeezed the young woman's hand, then she and Arno lifted the stretcher into the mobile clinic, shutting the doors behind them. The last thing this poor girl—Lerato—needed was a thousand eyes on her.

'There's so much blood,' Lerato winced, lifting her soaked skirt and letting out a wail that pierced Kaya's heart and made Arno look even more determined than he had just now, telling her what he would've done to her attacker if he'd caught him. With a rifle.

She was still reeling from the severity of his words, even though she knew he'd have done nothing of the sort—he wasn't that crazy. But he did just admit to her that he cared, and that he'd been thinking about it, stewing on it, imagining what he'd have done if he'd been there.

'When did you start bleeding?' she asked Lerato, pushing the conversation that had just been interrupted from her head. This girl had to be no older than fifteen.

'Last night,' the girl managed, pressing a hand to her belly, then screaming out. Arno had to restrain her from wriggling off the stretcher in pain. 'I had really bad pain the last few days. Cramps, back ache. I thought it was normal. Then I saw the blood.'

Kaya spotted her bloated belly and caught Arno's eye. She could tell he was thinking what she was: it was either appendicitis, or…she was pregnant.

So young, and pregnant?

Whatever it was, it was a miracle she was here. The poor girl had made her way to them unaccompanied. Apparently, a worried friend had told her that they were here. Five minutes later, and they might have already missed her. It didn't bear thinking about. Lerato looked disoriented now and complained that her shoulder was hurting worse than before. They studied her together under the lights. Arno's mouth was a grave, thin line.

'We'll have to check you,' Kaya explained, and the whole time they were helping her patiently through a blood and urine test she was hoping against hope that the girl *wasn't* pregnant. If she was, they couldn't give her much for the pain.

If she was, it might not have happened with her consent.

To Kaya's disappointment, the test was positive.

'She's so young,' she muttered to Arno over by the sink, and he shook his head, changing his gloves quickly without looking at her. He'd turned stone cold and silent, his concern for this girl mounting as much as hers, she assumed. The shoulder pain was a sign of internal bleeding... blood pooling in her abdomen. It was becoming evidently clear that Lerato was suffering a ruptured ectopic pregnancy. The baby inside her was already gone.

'Did you know you were pregnant?' she asked the tear-stained girl, helping Arno prepare the ultrasound.

'What?' The poor girl looked visibly shaken. 'No, no, no…'

Lerato was sniffling in both pain and what looked like confusion. The thought of how exactly she'd got pregnant so young was a whole other issue, but Arno was firing questions at her now, gently, kindly, in an effort to garner as much information as they could, while the girl crumbled in Kaya's arms and clung to her so tightly that Arno had to prise her off. The ultrasound confirmed she'd need surgery. Fifteen minutes later Arno was administering the anaesthesia.

The *beep-beep-beep* of the machines aligned with Kaya's own heartbeat. She was dutifully cool and collected on the surface, but the look on Arno's face told her this was serious, *and* that he wasn't impressed by whatever method this girl had come to be carrying a baby either.

'You'll feel better when you wake up,' Arno told the groggy girl gently, and while Kaya knew he was an expert, and had completed countless similar surgeries, she prayed he was right.

It was touch and go. With a ruptured fallopian tube, Lerato was losing a lot of blood. Kaya felt as if her own insides were being pulled taut as

Arno announced what she was quickly realising herself: 'Blood transfusion.'

'I was hoping you wouldn't say that.'

'So was I.'

Kaya sprang into action, thanking the heavens that Arno had ensured the mobile facility carried blood-draw, laboratory, and blood-storage equipment and they wouldn't have to call an air ambulance again. The space was smaller than any OR she'd ever stepped foot in; she could see the village kids outside, pressing their faces to the windows.

At times like this the hospital she'd been so used to back home felt far too far away, but this mobile operating room was even equipped to perform laparoscopic surgery; it had tools and cameras, and now she was more grateful than ever that Arno's diligence towards bringing the newest, best equipment to their remote patients, along with their skills, was his top priority.

How many people were injured after that fire at Nkosi Valley? she found herself wondering as they worked on the unfortunate unconscious girl. Arno, in blue scrubs, wore a look of iron indomitability, and looked visibly moved and even emotional as she cleaned the blood, and what was likely the unborn child.

It must take a lot to live through something like he had, she thought, and dedicate his life to saving lives as a result. Had he seen those three people who died in the restaurant, before it happened? Were they trying to get out? Had they died while he was trying to save them?

He must have seen so much, living out here. More than she ever had. Did it ever all get too much? At one point, she could have sworn she saw a damp tear slide from Arno's eye but she couldn't be sure. He was quick to swipe at his face and square his shoulders, and when he pulled off his gloves, leaving the girl to sleep off her anaesthesia, she asked him, 'Arno, are you OK?'

Kaya felt an unhindered urge to comfort him suddenly, and she didn't even quite know what for. He had an air about him now; something different. She could almost see his mind churning.

'I'm good,' he said bluntly, turning to wash his hands. She didn't believe him.

'I think we saved her,' she said, joining him at the sink, daring a sideways glance at his jawline as he pulled off his mask.

'I think so too.'

She frowned at the tap, scrubbing her hands. 'Have you…lost…many girls going through miscarriages here?' There had been articles and journals and statistics, of course, but now she wanted the truth from Arno's mouth; someone who'd been here for years, on the ground, witnessing it first-hand.

'Probably more than you've seen in the Netherlands, but less since we got Betsy on the road.' He turned to her, yanking a paper towel from the dispenser, then seemingly without thinking wiped at something on her cheek with it. 'And since we started hiring people like you,' he added, while her mind spun.

Her hand flattened over his, across her cheek. She was more embarrassed by what must have splattered on her face than concerned by the fact that he was touching her. For a second she clean forgot where they were.

This time, he didn't apologise, and Kaya didn't flinch or move away. This felt so new, so strange. Some kind of change to her DNA took her breath away as she scanned the depths of his eyes. Another chunk of the glacier crumbled away.

'Looks like we may have to postpone the presentation,' he said then, busying himself with the radio, which was buzzing for their attention, no doubt confirming a place for Lerato's recovery in the nearest medical facility. 'We'll have to drive her to the hospital.'

'I don't want to leave her, anyway,' Kaya said, aware of how his touch had left her slightly breathless and flustered. Her hands shook as she pulled her hair from the bun and re-bundled it on top of her head. 'She came here alone, Arno. I need to find out her story. Young teenage girls don't just… Do you think she was…?'

The word left such a bad taste in her mouth that she couldn't get it out. As she turned to their patient, hooked to the IV, the memories of her own attacker were crashing back in now: the bulk of his body over hers on the cold mud, pinning her down, her whole life flashing before her eyes. The way she'd dragged herself home to Pieter, who'd forced her back out to the police station, where she'd been treated like just another statistic who'd been in the wrong place at the wrong time.

'I can't leave her till I know,' she whispered now, determination ebbing like an ever-expanding river through her bones. If she could help another victim find justice, or peace, or both, she'd do whatever it took.

'Breathe.' Arno put his hands to her shoulders, forcing her back to the moment. In spite of the tension between them, which was always there, no matter *what* the situation apparently, she found comfort instantly in his gaze, and she took a deep breath while he steadied her.

'I understand,' he said, tilting her chin. 'Kaya, we'll find out what happened, I promise.'

In that moment, she was overcome with relief

that she'd told him what happened to her. He *did* understand why being here for this girl was important to her, and he was on her side.

CHAPTER TEN

FROM THE COLD plastic seats in the bleach-white waiting room, Arno watched Kaya taking in the modest clinic, which admittedly was only marginally better equipped than their vehicle, Betsy. Their young patient Lerato was stable, hooked to a new IV, in a bed of her own, but, of course, Kaya wouldn't leave until they'd spoken to a relative.

They'd been here two hours already. He was famished and exhausted, but no way was he leaving without her, and without knowing the girl would be OK. He kept sneaking glances at Kaya, aware of every time she adjusted her hair or twiddled her hands, trying not to look whenever she tapped at her phone. This was the first time they'd had a signal in a few days. Maybe she was texting her boyfriend.

He'd been trying—and failing—not to let that bother him. It'd been a long time since he'd experienced anything like jealousy and it didn't sit well. What would he have done with her anyway? Had a fling, before she disappeared from his life for ever? He snorted to himself. That was ridiculous. Kaya was so far off fling material it wasn't even funny. She was...special.

Maybe it was a good thing she wasn't single; it was getting harder to be around her without wanting to break every single rule he'd ever set for himself about making moves on volunteers.

Just then, the door blew open and a torpedo in the shape of a man, no older than seventeen or eighteen, came charging through. 'Where is she? Where's Lerato?' He looked as if he'd run a thousand miles; perspiration soaked his baseball hat and flapping shirt.

Kaya was on her feet in a heartbeat. Arno followed after her. 'How do you know Lerato?' she demanded, stopping in front of him so fast her shoes squeaked on the tiles.

'Where is she? Is she OK?' the guy urged her, putting his arms out to grab her in his desperation.

Kaya staggered backwards, just as Arno caught his forearms, holding him tightly away from her. 'It's OK,' he assured him, calmly, as Kaya composed herself at his side. 'No need to panic, Lerato is fine. Who are you?'

'I'm Navi, I'm her boyfriend!'

The commotion, now being witnessed by two

doctors, a nurse and three other patients, seemed to have stirred the sleeping Lerato awake. She started calling his name. 'Navi! Navi, is that you?'

Navi pushed past them all and one of the doctors let him into the room. Kaya followed, peeking suspiciously through the glass door, and Arno's heartbeat regulated itself as it became pretty clear the two did indeed know each other.

'They're a couple,' Kaya whispered, nodding at the way Navi was cradling the now-crying Lerato, sitting at her bedside, swiping back tears. Lerato was gripping his shirt the way you only did if you never wanted someone to let go. Kaya wasn't even pretending to hide her relief that the pregnancy had been an accident involving two loved-up teens, and not some kind of violation, and he bit back a smile.

'Looks like they're pretty close,' he confirmed as another jolt of something like jealousy shook his senses—this time for the kind of love he'd never even got halfway close to having himself. He'd been too busy since Bea—telling himself he was too busy—but the truth was, he just didn't trust himself or his past not to mess it up.

Kaya was looking at him strangely now. He realised he'd been staring at her again, tracing the outline of her mouth with his eyes, lost in thought. Gosh, he was so tired, and all his bones ached, but they still had a pretty long drive.

'They are most definitely a committed boy-friend and girlfriend,' Kaya said. 'Even if they're far too young and probably need a lesson on the dangers of unprotected sex.'

The dusty road stretched ahead of them as he steered towards Thabisa. Streaks from the hot, setting sun were starting to turn the sky into a coal pit of burning red embers above them. Eventually his growling stomach forced him to stop at a resting post that served them both grilled chicken, while Kaya talked about her plans for adding sexual-health awareness and sex education to her school presentations in future.

He nodded and murmured in the appropriate places, wondering how much more she'd take on. The garden was already a talking point—every community for miles that didn't have one already wanted to speed up planting one with the foundation's help.

He also couldn't help thinking she was filling every bit of silence on purpose, in case the awkward tension crept back in. In a way he was grateful she was taking the job off his hands. There hadn't ever been a volunteer he'd experienced this level of attraction to. Not only was it wholly inappropriate, but knowing she was taken added a whole other element to his predicament.

Back on the road, the silence enveloped them

and, as predicted, felt awkward. If she felt this attraction too, which he assumed she did, judging by her body language and the way she flushed red every time they locked eyes, or hands, she was probably feeling a little conflicted because of her boyfriend back home. Whoever he was. Lucky guy.

'Mud bath?' Kaya exclaimed suddenly, wrinkling her nose as they whizzed past the creaky old sign that marked the start of the old dirt track.

He smirked, stifling a yawn. 'Don't knock it till you've tried it.'

'Are you serious?'

Arno slowed the vehicle. The thought of a cool, relaxing mud bath right now was actually not a terrible one. 'It's good for your skin,' he said. 'Like a mineral mask. There are lots of them around. But only a few that aren't occupied by hippos.'

Kaya laughed; the first time he'd heard her laugh all day. In a moment of spontaneity he could only attribute to his exhaustion, he pulled a U-turn and rumbled the vehicle back towards the sign.

Since the time she'd been caught out and had to meet Arno's mother looking like a mud-splattered hurricane victim, Kaya had been careful to pack a change of clothes with her on every remote round.

She pulled out her spare bra and knickers now, glancing back at Arno from behind the scraggy bush, suddenly more self-aware than ever. He had to be the hottest creature to ever exist, and now he was pulling his shirt over his head, showing off those tight abs and slick stomach to absolutely no one intentionally, kicking out of his trousers, stepping into a pair of boxer shorts.

Oh, my God.

Kaya gasped as she caught a momentary glimpse of his round bare bum, whiter than white, like the moon against a sepia twilight. Committing it to memory for ever took less than a millisecond—it was without doubt the nicest bum to ever accidentally fall into her eyeline.

'Are you OK behind there?' he called now, yanking his bathing shorts up and turning around. Quickly she slid back behind the bush, hurrying on with her navy-blue underwear, glad it matched and wasn't too transparent, a giddy grin breaking out on her face. OK, so it wasn't a bikini, but was matching underwear better or worse? She must be totally exhausted and maybe a bit crazy after the heat and drama of the day, to agree to this.

Or maybe she was just besotted with a man she couldn't have? Clearly both. Why else would she have agreed to do something as potentially dangerous as taking a mud bath in the middle of nowhere?

'Are you sure there are no hippos?' she asked, stepping out into the clearing, still in her boots. She forced her arms not to hug her body out of Arno's view, and felt the wickedness seep further through her bloodstream till she was practically fizzing in his gaze. It felt good, actually, to be admired by him. Anyone else looking at her like...*this*...would probably have made her run a mile.

'Blue suits you,' he said now, without answering her question, and she watched his eyes rove like flashlights from her feet to her face. For just a moment, it looked as if he couldn't tear his eyes away. Thank goodness she'd kept up with her Pilates and kickboxing back in Amsterdam. It had all been an effort to keep her strong, and boost her confidence, but the results were evident in everything she wore...and didn't wear.

Was that a mild groan she heard from Arno's throat as he marched on ahead of her, telling her to stay close? She bit back another smile. Whatever was happening to her, it was definitely interesting. When was the last time she'd felt this alive?

'We're fenced in,' Arno explained, when he'd

found his voice. 'The mud bath is part of the last village we passed. We're safe, trust me.'

Kaya studied his sculpted bare back and shoulders as he swiped at grass and branches ahead of her, and considered how the width equalled strength, and wondered if he'd carried anyone out of that fire he seemed to hate talking about so much. He'd only been eighteen. He carried them still, she thought—those people who lost their lives. He was troubled. Maybe that was why she was drawn to him, really.

Trouble invites trouble.

She'd been so determined not to feed her silly crush on him lately that she had perhaps come off a little cold herself since that night when they'd talked in the barn. No wonder he assumed he'd crossed a line and upset her.

Now that was behind them, thankfully, but the air was far from clear. You could slit it with an army knife the second things went quiet, which was why she'd done her best to make small talk about anything and everything till now—so much so that her throat was sore. It took a lot of effort to seem cool, when your heart was doing a tap dance.

'OK…time for your mud bath, milady,' he said from ahead of her, sweeping aside a final curtain of green foliage and beckoning her on past him.

His hand brushed the skin across her lower

back as she crossed the threshold; the lightest, slightest touch intended only to guide her across the rough ground in her boots, but the skin-on-skin contact sent another bolt to her lady parts that she definitely had not been expecting. When was the last time a man touched her at all, while she'd been wearing so little? Arno would be shocked if he knew, no doubt about that. And she would be humiliated. Which was why she'd never, ever tell him.

'This is it?' she asked him, stopping just ahead of him. He walked up alongside her, studying the grey-brown pool of mud at their feet, surrounded by dust and dirt and fallen leaves and branches.

'This is it. It gets bigger after the rains,' he said, crouching down to the pool. It must be no more than six-foot squared, she thought, watching him scoop a handful of the gloopy substance into one palm and smear a little on one arm. How did he get all these muscles? she wondered as the late sun danced along the contours of his shoulder blades. There was a small gym at the resort, she supposed, and he did seem to wake up earlier than most people, most mornings. She knew because she'd seen him from time to time, going out to meet Tande, no doubt. Did he work out before or after that? What did he look like in gym gear? Maybe he did it shirtless. Maybe she should work out one morning and find out.

'Want some?' he asked her, interrupting her reverie.

Kaya blinked. 'That is why we're here,' she replied quickly as he stood, holding the mud in his hand between them. 'What do we do with it exactly?' she asked him, touching a finger to the squidgy goo.

'You cover yourself in it.' He smirked, as if she amused him. 'Like a hippo.'

'Are you calling me a hippo?' The flirtatious question slipped straight from her mouth as she bent and scooped some mud for herself, then flicked it at him.

'Hey!' Arno let out a laugh of surprise, which only set her off, too. A glob of sticky mud had landed straight on his neck, and no sooner had he smudged it in than he was flinging some back at her. Another giant glob landed right on her chest above her left breast and when she looked up, she realised he'd been watching her rub it in, smudging more mud across his own torso. Another spike of adrenaline tore through her.

The mini mud fight lasted less than a minute; it was hard to move when the stuff was sticking to her in every place she could imagine, but when a fresh glob trickled down her forehead and into her eyes, Arno stepped forward and reached a hand to her face; then, quick as a flash, pulled it back again, as if he was physically restraining himself from touching her.

Disappointment coursed through her veins. She turned her back, feeling his eyes on her as she covered her legs, one by one. *Look, but don't touch*—that was the vibe here. For both of them.

It wasn't as if she'd given Arno any reason to believe that the whole time she'd been actively keeping her distance from him, she'd been thinking about his hands in hers, and his arms around her, and just generally imagining what it would be like to sleep in a man's arms again—specifically his.

He'd been making her think all kinds of things lately, like how it would feel to actually trust someone implicitly after so long, knowing they only had her best interests at heart. Wouldn't it be nice to feel protected and safe with a man, instead of repulsed and/or terrified? It wasn't so hard to imagine all that whenever she looked at Arno… It felt as though another old demon got incinerated every time she laughed with him, or opened up, but he knew she was damaged. She'd told him about the attack and while it was nice knowing he'd been thinking about it, so much so that he'd imagined exacting some kind of bitter vengeance on her behalf, even if they weren't colleagues, with a certifiably big difference in age, he knew she wasn't someone he could ever really get close to. She didn't belong here, for a start.

Still…it might be high time to change the way people looked at her, she thought, and, come to think of it, the way she'd been looking at herself for far too long.

CHAPTER ELEVEN

THE MUD WAS cool relief across her skin, the more Kaya coated her arms, neck and stomach with it. Within minutes they were sitting side by side on the edge of the small pool, caked in the stuff like two happy hippos.

'Kaolinite, bentonite, magnesium, potassium, and all kinds of other stuff,' Arno explained, after she'd asked exactly what it was that was now crackling across her skin in the day's heat, still radiating off the ground. 'It gets rid of all impurities.'

She caught his eyes then, and he took a huge lungful of air and blew it out through his teeth at the sinking sun. 'Well, maybe not *all* impurities,' he added wryly.

Kaya's throat went tight. The air was thicker than the mud now. If she shuffled one centimetre closer to him, she could kiss him. She could actually feel his lips on hers, mud or no mud, if she wanted, if she dared…

She held her breath as he rested on his elbows next to her. Did he just imply that he was thinking impure thoughts about her? Or did she read that completely wrong? Hmmm. This wasn't something she was used to, exactly. Usually that kind of sexual objectification would send a storm of terror and horror and indignation raging round her skull and out of her mouth, but now she was kind of curious, and quietly turned on.

'I heard mud can also stimulate blood flow,' she said now, daring to study the trail of coarse, mud-coated hair down from his navel, straight into the waistline of his boxers as he kept his face turned to the sky.

'Affirmative,' he replied after a moment, glancing her way for a split second. She bit down on her lip, swallowed back her pounding heart from her throat.

'So, Kaya.' He folded his arms behind his head on the ground.

She braced herself.

'What does your boyfriend think about you being all the way out here? With me?'

'What?' Her heart skipped a beat, then started racing; where on earth did he get the impression she was in a relationship? The thought was almost laughable. She hugged her knees, the shock making her smile. 'I don't have a boyfriend!'

His eyebrows shot skywards. Then he turned

to her, resting on one elbow, giving her his full attention. Behind him, three young kids hovered around a fence, as if they were contemplating interrupting them. For a second she prayed they would. The way Arno was looking at her now was so intense, almost as if he were probing her mind with his eyes.

'Why would you think that?' she followed carefully.

He drew a line in the mud between them with one finger, then looked up at her through his eyelashes. 'Back there, in the village, you said your boyfriend never went out and tried to find who did that to you, in the park.'

A deep frown cracked the mud around his forehead and she wondered how long he'd been stewing over this. A small thrill pierced through her reluctance to talk about it.

'I did have a boyfriend when it happened,' she admitted. 'What I meant was…well, it doesn't matter now, does it? It ended. Pieter ended things, about a year ago.'

Arno sat up next to her, mirrored her knee-hugging stance. 'Sorry,' he said. 'It's none of my business.'

'It's OK.' Kaya brushed at the hardened mud on her arms, watching the kids turn the other way and scramble back along a pathway, followed by a dog. What must they look like, sitting here like this? Suddenly she was all self-conscious again, solo in Arno's scrutiny. But she found herself talking anyway.

'Things weren't the same after the attack.' She sighed, fighting the urge to hide or run, as she always did. 'Pieter wanted me to act like I had before and I just…couldn't.'

'I get it,' Arno said, nodding darkly at the pond.

'It was like something froze in me. I didn't want him, or anyone to…'

'I get it,' he said again, and the gravity of his tone silenced her.

Did he? Did he really get it? She wasn't going to spell it out—that she hadn't been able to get intimate with her ex. Or that she'd moved in with her parents, or that Pieter went on to cheat on her with one of her friends from work.

Ugh, it had all made her feel so bad, as if she were less of a woman somehow. She'd carried that thought for three whole years, till now. Till someone had looked at her as Arno was looking at her now.

The sun was sinking like a melting ball of fire. Orange hues stained the sky and brought flecks of gold to his eyes. Now her crush had multiplied by a hundred thousand, and she was sure he could see it.

'I know what it's like to feel a bit broken,'

he said after a moment. 'After the fire, things weren't the same with my parents. I felt like everyone was judging me.' He paused and Kaya's curiosity spiked as high as her heart rate. He hardly ever talked about the fire, or how it must have affected him.

'I felt like everyone was looking at me differently,' he continued.

'But why? The fire wasn't your fault,' she said, releasing her knees. 'How could you have stopped it, even if you had been there? Those other people tried, and they couldn't stop it.'

'I could have got Mama Annika out sooner,' he said. 'She was my responsibility. She was p—'

He shut his mouth, as if he'd suddenly said too much, then sighed through his teeth again, getting to his feet. 'We should wash this mud off and get back,' he said, holding a hand down to her.

Without thinking she took it, letting him pull her up, and suddenly they were face to face like two muddy monsters emerging from a swamp. Maybe it was the mud blocking every other feature on his face, but his eyes held more intensity, more bottled-up emotion than she'd ever seen, as they stood there, his hand still firmly in hers.

'Mama Annika was what?'

'The past is the past,' he interjected, as if he could possibly erase all the questions about *his* past that were spinning like a merry-go-round in her brain. 'What I meant to say was, I wish to hell that didn't have to happen to you, Kaya.'

One side of his mouth curved into a self-deprecating smile as he traced her mouth with his eyes. 'I shouldn't say this, but I'm also kind of glad you're single, too.'

Kaya was so shocked she let out a sound that was half gasp, half laugh, and turned her face to the ground. Thank goodness she was covered in mud, so he couldn't see her blushing.

'No, you shouldn't say things like that,' she agreed quietly, but she let him hold her hand the whole way back along the path to their vehicle, under the mutual guise of him leading the way. She even let him hose the mud off her back with the mobile unit's water supply and he did so slowly, carefully, as if it was his one main mission to have her emerge fresh, clean, his own personal achievement. She'd felt so wanted and desired, and so impossibly changed from the woman she'd been just a few weeks ago.

There was one moment, when she was washing the mud off his broad shoulders from behind, when time seemed to slow right down. It was only them, two normal, unbroken individuals enjoying the sensuous act of washing each other…right before he seemed to trip clumsily on the hosepipe and right himself, as if he was so distracted by her being there that he'd lost his balance.

It all made her feel seen, and attractive, and hopeful in a way she hadn't in ages. Damn this crush. OK, so he felt it too, clearly, but it wasn't as if either of them were in a position to do anything about it. He knew he shouldn't. He'd said it. *She* knew they shouldn't... They were here to work, not flirt.

Neither of them went any deeper than small talk on the drive back to Thabisa but her heart was like a wild zebra bucking in her chest, every single time Arno looked her way. She couldn't help the smiles breaking out on her face, and she didn't miss his either, no matter how much he might be trying to bite them back.

When they were finally back at the resort, the sun had set fully on the day and the volunteers eyed them in interest from their camping chairs around the fire pit. She was still fighting the urge to ask him more about the night of the fire; something told her there was more to it than him showing up drunk and too late. Something about Mama Annika that he'd been about to tell her and held back on. Maybe she should search online—he was bound to come up. But no, that didn't feel right. If he didn't want her to know something, he must have his reasons.

Besides, the Internet out here was terrible.

'Where have you two been all day?' the Australian lady, Kimberley, called out, urging her over. Kaya watched Arno slink away like a cat and fought not to let the disappointment overshadow her good mood as she took a seat. Someone was playing guitar. The others were chatting quietly.

'We had an emergency, in one of the villages. Arno had to operate,' she whispered, searching for him in the shadows.

Kimberley frowned at her suspiciously in the firelight. 'What's that on your cheek?' she asked suddenly. 'And in your hair!'

'Oh.' Kaya brought a hand to her face, touching a patch of crusty mud she'd clearly just missed in her haphazard flirt-fest back at the mud bath. Obviously it was still caked in her hair too—it wasn't as if they'd had shampoo.

'Did you fall in a river?'

'Not exactly. We went to a mud bath.'

'*We?*' Kimberley lowered her voice conspiratorially. 'You mean, Dr Nkosi took you for a spa treatment?'

'It was an outdoor mud bath,' she explained, compressing her lips and folding her arms over herself to cover any more unfortunate splatters that might have made it onto her clothing when she'd put it back on. 'As in, *natural*. It's not like we went to a *spa*.'

God, how did this look to the others? Not good, probably.

'Look at you, getting all the special treatment.' Kimberley bit her lip. 'Maybe I should ask if we can all go get a spa treatment tomorrow, huh?'

Kaya shuffled in her seat, wishing she'd just gone straight to her room and washed her hair, as Arno probably did. 'It wasn't like that, it was just there, on the way back.'

'It doesn't exactly sound part of the package.' Kimberley was only teasing her the way anyone would if they discovered their colleagues might be hooking up, but Kaya didn't miss the beer cans around the fire, the way Kimberley was loose in her seat now, as if she might swivel off it at any moment and fall. How long had they been drinking?

'What's going on?'

Kaya's stomach dropped as one of the guys got up from his chair and crossed to them, waving a beer can. Mark from Canterbury, a tall, lanky med student who wanted to be a dentist, was renowned for being the more vocal amongst the volunteers at the best of times. 'Did I hear something about you and Arno? Are the rumours true?'

Rumours? Kaya swallowed, getting up from her seat.

'I think they might be. First she gets to stay

the night at his winery. Now she's going for mud baths with him…'

Kaya cringed as they talked between themselves as though she weren't there.

It was harmless fun, but clearly they'd been talking about her and Arno all this time, and probably thought they were doing more than they actually were. Plus, they were way too drunk for her to be comfortable.

Kaya turned to go, but Mark had other ideas.

'Ah, come on, Kaya! Stay with us. You're always such a stick-in-the-*mud*—get it?'

'I have to go, it's been a long day,' she insisted as her defences rose like a drawbridge at his proximity.

'Have some fun with us! Or are you saving all that for your alone time with the doctor?'

He caught her elbow. She pulled away but he did it again, trying to make her stay, and suddenly his leering face in the firelight was all she could see. Kaya froze, feeling the tears flood her eyes as the flashbacks assaulted her one by one. The teeth up close, the odour of alcohol on his breath, the clammy hands…she was back there.

Kimberley was cackling from her chair. Mark was trying to dance with her now, telling her he was only teasing her, wrapping an arm around her waist. Her feet wouldn't move; he was that man in the park, all over again, leering and jeering and smelling of booze…

'Get your hands off her!'

The booming voice sounded out like a bomb behind them, shaking her to her senses. Arno stormed towards them and past her like an angry bear, and suddenly she was free and Mark was staggering backwards, hands in the air, beer spilling everywhere.

'I heard you all, acting like animals,' Arno seethed. 'What the hell are you doing? Are you drunk?' His eyes scanned the circle and she watched him take in the beer cans, the scattered biscuits and discarded plates. Everyone was on their feet now, stunned into a sheepish silence. She'd never seen him so angry.

'Are you guys serious? Is this what happens when I leave the property? This isn't some kind of party!'

'We were just…' Kimberley trailed off, awkwardly.

'You were just *drinking*.' Arno glowered, swiping up a can, then tossing it hard into the blazing fire, which spat in instant disapproval. 'Did I not specifically state when you all arrived that we don't drink here, not in the week, not when we have patients to see first thing in the morning, people who might *need* us?'

The group muttered their apologies as Arno

simmered. Kaya could tell he was doing his best to swallow the rage that had just consumed him.

'They were just having a bit of fun,' she tried, although she could still feel Mark's hands on her; and everything that 'bit of fun' had thrown to the forefront of her memories. He'd held her so tightly just now, the white marks from his hand on her flesh had turned to red.

Arno wasn't looking at her. He was glowering at Mark, who was backing off towards the rooms slowly, as you'd try to escape a rhino itching to pierce your lungs with a lethal horn. She put a hand to Arno's arm gently. 'Arno, it's all right.'

'Are *you* all right?' he said now, turning to her in front of everyone.

She nodded mutely, rubbing her arms, then remembered to stand tall. She'd done nothing wrong; let people talk, let people think what they wanted about her—*them*. She was done being some precious flower, stuck in the shadows. And Mark should not have put his hands on her under any circumstances—he knew that. She could tell he was already regretting it.

Arno's face was still dark as a storm cloud.

'Everyone out of here, now,' Arno barked, and the group scattered on command, till it was just the two of them, standing by the fire in the dark.

'I saw his hands on you,' Arno hissed into the crackling fire. 'I saw red.' He sank to a chair, kicked another can and pressed his hands to his head. She didn't know what to do, except touch a hand to his shoulder from behind him. Somehow it felt as if it was Arno who needed comforting right now.

She helped him clean up the cans, while he muttered things about how much he loathed drinking, how it ruined everything, how he shouldn't have overreacted. She bit her tongue. From what he'd said earlier, he blamed himself— a little—for being out drinking when that fire broke out at the winery. It made sense, why he'd overreacted, but he'd also been worried about her. It was everything combined.

This thing, whatever it was, was growing between them, stronger by the minute. Maybe he was as frustrated as she was.

As he walked her back to her room, Kaya toyed with the notion that once the panic over Mark's behaviour had subsided, and Arno had appeared to defend her honour, she'd probably never felt so turned on in her life. This was all so confusing.

'Get some sleep, you must be exhausted,' he said, swiping at his eyes on her doorstep.

'Thank you, for tonight,' she replied, hoping he knew what that meant. She got lost in his eyes in the light from the porch, wishing the night wouldn't have to end. A distant cry of a night bird pierced the air and he squeezed his eyes closed, pretending to bang his head against the door.

'I shouldn't have been such an ogre with them.' He winced against the wood. 'They'll hate me now.'

'No, they won't. They'll respect you even more.'

'Drinking against my rules is one thing, I can forgive that, I know they were just letting loose, but when I saw Mark's hands on you, after what you said, what you had to go through...'

She stepped towards him, courage pushing her to the tips of his toes. 'That's the funny thing about having someone's hands on me. If it's *you*, I really don't mind.'

Kaya touched a palm to his cheek, caressing the softness of his face, allowing one finger to sweep his cheekbone before he covered her hand with his. The warmth of him washed deliciously over her fingers and she swore she could feel his pulse quicken. She'd read a study once that said that when a person was attracted to another, their heartbeat synchronised with that of their lover. It wasn't just science, it was chemistry. This was something she had *never* felt this strongly. Not even with Pieter at the start.

Kaya drew a jagged breath as his eyes narrowed speculatively. 'What about if I kissed you? Would you mind that?'

'I don't know.' Nervous excitement pulsed through her, like a million fingers tickling her heart and belly. She rested her hand against his heart, stepped closer till her hips were pressed to his. 'You can always try?'

Arno traced a feather-light thumb over her lower lip, and she swallowed against the sensation of her heart skyrocketing up to her trachea and getting stuck there.

'Do you trust me?' he asked her, his mouth so close she could almost taste it already.

Her fingers found the fabric of his shirt. Arno ran his hand caressingly over the curve of her waist and she clean forgot where they were as he bent to kiss her. Time stopped when his lips landed on hers…softly, gently, as if he was testing the waters. And while it was a much lighter kiss than she actually desired, hunger throbbed and shot through her loins, making her gasp for a breath.

'Maybe we shouldn't.' Arno groaned, releasing her, obviously mistaking her rush of desire and pleasure for another disturbing flashback.

A rapid pulse beat a new song in her throat. A dull ache nagged at her insides as she reached for him, and dared to press her lips to his again, opening her mouth this time, welcoming his tongue. Just the smallest flick of it against hers was enough to breathe new life into her. Just one sensual touch between tongues made her feel as if she were shooting back to the surface after months underwater. A ripple of laughter escaped her throat and she clutched fistfuls of his shirt, pressed her forehead to his heart, relieved she could still do it, that she could still kiss and be kissed, and enjoy it.

'Was that too much?' he asked her now, and she shook her head.

'It wasn't enough.' She smiled into him, releasing a sigh into his chest as his big arms looped around her. They stayed that way a moment, in a spill of moonlight that felt almost magical to Kaya, until Arno prised her hands away, moved to the steps of the porch.

'Get some sleep,' he said again from the step below her, curling a lick of muddy hair behind her ear. This time she was the one to emit a groan. He was leaving. Correctly so—this was already a disaster waiting to happen. But by the look of his trousers now, he wanted more, too.

'If I stay one second more, I will do something I might regret,' he said, confirming her thoughts. He scooped her by the nape of her neck, and pressed his lips to her forehead this time, leaving a hot trail of tingles in his wake. Looking deep into his eyes, she saw how much he wanted her, but in seconds he had disappeared into the night, leaving her breathless on the porch, haunted by the taste of him.

CHAPTER TWELVE

'KAYA, I NEED YOU!' Arno shoved the radio back in its holder and held a hand up at her over the ruckus of teens all clamouring around her, outside the school.

'What's up?' she said, heading his way in her uniform blue T-shirt, swatting a fly from her face while a teenager talked at her a million miles an hour. He watched the sun play on her cheekbones as Kaya took her shoulder gently. 'Honey, I'll be back very soon, you can ask me any more questions then.'

She was good with kids, whatever their age. It was hard not to notice.

'Looks like there's been a road accident up ahead. We're the closest medics, we need to go now,' he said gravely, opening the Jeep door and resisting the impulse to put a hand to her back or steady her as she climbed up quickly, issuing a hurried goodbye to the girl, who was *still* trying to talk to her about her boyfriend.

They'd just given the presentation at the school that had been postponed a week ago, and the bit about safe sex, by Kaya herself, had sparked a barrage of questions that he'd done his best to answer, but let Kaya handle for the most part. Now it looked as if they were needed for something more pressing. Hopefully it wasn't too serious.

In seconds he was swerving out of the school-yard and Kaya was gripping the handle.

'I'll never get used to your driving.' She grimaced as he hurtled through a puddle, and he battled a laugh at the look on her face, told her she would *have* to get used to it eventually, then realised she probably wouldn't, seeing as she was leaving at the end of her six-month placement.

Which was exactly the reason he hadn't made another move on her since that kiss last week. Why go down that path with a volunteer?

It wasn't easy, staying professional, when all he wanted to do was taste more of her. The other night, when the November rains had slashed his windows and kept him awake, he'd wanted to go to her so badly, but then, she hadn't made another move either. So here they were, at some kind of torturous stalemate that thickened the air every time they were in the same room…or Jeep. Like now.

A female in her mid-twenties, who'd been established as Sarah from the UK, was sitting on the roadside when they pulled up. A smashed-up hire car lay smoking on its side in the vines. Officer Marlo—whom Arno had known for years—ran at them from the overturned car, shouting something about the back seat. Sarah was crying uncontrollably, clutching her stomach and chest.

'There's someone in the back seat,' Marlo panted, sending Arno's heart straight up to his mouth. 'Her partner, Daniel. I couldn't get the door open. Looks like there's blood.'

Arno grabbed his backpack, told Kaya to stay with Sarah. The girl was sobbing wretched sobs, struggling for air. Whiplash from the seat belt was evident on her skin, but there could well be internal bleeding. Kaya would check.

'He wasn't wearing a seat belt,' he heard Sarah sob, and dread seized Arno's chest as he peered through the broken window. The guy, Daniel, lay whimpering in shock on the back seat. Marlo was right; blood had soaked his white shirt and pooled onto the seat. He pulled at the twisted door, but it was no good. Running to the other side, he tried the other one and yelped as broken glass slashed his hand.

Dammit.

'It's not moving,' he yelled at Marlo as Kaya ran over to assist. Quickly he hid his bleeding hand from her. He would address that later. Getting this guy out was imperative. Kaya went for the door handle, but he darted in front of her. 'Kaya, no, there's too much glass…'

'I want to help,' she told him. 'Sarah is stable. What do we do? Where are the first responders?'

'We are the first responders,' he said, checking the mangled back window now. 'The roads are too narrow. Look, this might be our only way in.'

Stepping over broken glass and twisted vines, Arno picked up part of a broken fence post, assessing the best way to use it to get into the car. Kaya followed him to the back, one hand over her mouth. Behind them, Sarah was hugging her knees ten feet away, rocking like a baby, but at least she was fine and conscious.

The car was smoking profusely now. Marlo was still tugging at the other back door. Inside, Daniel groaned, his face pale, shrouded in smoke.

'They were drinking. These damn wine tourists, it's always the same,' Marlo growled, before cursing loudly at the jammed door again. 'No idea what they're messing with, coming out here…'

'Help me with this,' Arno barked, tossing him another piece of fencepost. He ordered Kaya to stand back as they took the wooden posts to the remaining back windscreen. He bit his tongue as his thumb throbbed with the impact, but Kaya was ready with blankets, fearlessly shoving them against the jagged edges, creating a smooth exit.

'We need to be fast,' he told them both, but the pain in his hand was unreal now. Scarlet blood oozed from his thumb down his wrist.

Ignore it. You're fine.

'Arno, I'll crawl in, I'm the smallest,' Kaya said now, making for the hole they'd just forged in the back of the car. He barred her with his good arm.

'No.'

'Let me!'

'No.'

There was no way he was letting her in this vehicle, not on his watch. He was already fighting the memories of the arms flailing from the restaurant windows that night—the giant restaurant that was already too choked for three people to escape from. He might be wounded now but he was still the strongest. She battled his decision with narrowed eyes and he turned from her before he broke, and scrambled through the window to the back seat.

Smoke made his eyes water as he assessed the damage up close in the tiny space. No time to linger. Daniel was conscious but the blood was pooling from his upper-left chest area—he had to keep him talking.

'Stay with me, you're fine. Tell me the date,

tell me your girlfriend's name… Kaya, get me something to tie round him,' he called out.

Kaya pushed another sheet towards him. Good enough. 'Left upper anterior open chest wound,' he told her as her face appeared in the shattered window to his side.

'Arno, hurry up!'

She didn't have to tell him that. Making a quick job with the makeshift occlusive dressing, he clocked the open bottle of wine in the back seat, and the rest of the bottles that had been thrown and smashed in the accident. There was enough booze in here to spark an inferno.

An angry hissing sound from somewhere near the front of the car sent his mind reeling back to that night—the black-as-night smoke clamouring for oxygen from the restaurant windows, shattered glass, employees on their knees, calling for the ones they'd lost, Mama Annika gasping for breath as he pulled her out, the sirens wailing in the distance. Adrenaline claimed his throat with the acrid smoke as he hoisted Daniel onto his lap.

Kaya and Marlo took his arms. Daniel slumped, a heavyweight against his chest, and Arno willed the pain away from his own throbbing hand as he handed Daniel out to them as steadily and quickly as he could.

'Get him away from here,' he yelled at them, clutching his hand as the car made an ominous creaking sound. The memories rushed at him; seeing his mother, running in drunk and stumbling, dragging her out on the strength of pure willpower, just before the roaring fire shot through her bedroom.

Focus, focus, focus, Arno.

Kaya and Marlo were running, dragging Daniel between them towards Sarah. Heaving himself through the window again, clutching his bloodied arm, Arno had barely made it three steps from the wreckage when the car burst into flames.

Kaya used her body as a shield. Crouching over Sarah and Daniel, she and Marlo dropped to the ground as the heat from the explosion threatened to scald them all. A distant siren wailed. A woman in a red dress she didn't recognise was rushing towards them now through the vineyard, arms in the air, but she kept losing her in the smoke.

'Arno.' She coughed, searching the wreckage for him with her eyes. 'Arno?' She stood on wobbly legs. Where was Arno?

Fear took her entire body hostage. The siren wailed closer, louder, louder than the crackling fire that was now burning wildly where the car had been. He was still inside?

'No, no, no…' Tears flooded her eyes, and

burned like the smoke. She scanned the scene for him. Did he make it out? Oh, God…no… surely not…

Then, there he was, staggering towards her, like a superhero at the end of an action movie! All the breath left her body as she met him in the middle of the road and threw her arms around him, just as a fire truck and an ambulance screeched up beside them. Arno let her hold him in a blur of firemen and hoses and paramedics and spraying water; let her inspect him, let her lead him over to the others and sit him by the roadside. He was breathless, weaker than she'd ever seen from breathing all that smoke.

'I'll help you to the ambulance,' she said. His face was black as soot, his shirt was ashen and bloodied. Daniel's blood?

No, *his* blood.

'I don't need them, I have you,' he managed, and she stared at him helplessly. Blood was streaming from his hand.

Kaya grappled for the med kit on the ground, hands shaking. Behind them the fire was almost out. Daniel was being strapped to a stretcher, while Officer Marlo seemed to be explaining something to the woman in red, who'd run to the scene through the vineyard. She looked distressed to say the least. The car was now a mangled black wreck, steaming into the bright blue sky. They were all lucky to be alive.

When she got him to the Jeep, Arno slid to the ground at the wheel, catching his breath, pressing the oxygen mask to his own mouth till the colour flushed back to his cheeks again. Her heart made a lump in her throat as she cleaned out his wound, checking for shards of glass, all the while giving the paramedic who approached them as much info as she could about what just happened.

'You might need stitches,' she told Arno, when he'd gone.

'I'm fine,' he mouthed, through the inhaler.

'You're not fine. We should go with them to the hospital.'

He tore the mask from his face. 'It's not that bad, Kaya, I'm telling you. I don't need that.'

She scowled at him, pulling the bandage tighter, making him suck in a grimace through his teeth. 'Stubborn idiot,' she snapped, standing up as the tears sprang back into her eyes. 'You scared the crap out of me.'

'I'd rather scare you than let you crawl in a car that's about to blow!'

Arno clenched his good fist, and she bit back her next words about it being OK for him, but not for her. Swiping at her face, she cursed under her breath, turned to the sky.

Breathe, Kaya. He was trying to protect you.

Her emotions were getting the better of her. She cared so much about him and hadn't been able to do a single thing about it since that kiss. They hadn't even mentioned it since. It was killing her. They shouldn't have let things get so messed up. Of course she'd be the one to suffer—*of course* he didn't want to start something with a volunteer, and neither should she, but it didn't mean she could switch off her feelings.

'Kaya.' He reached for her now, urged her down to his level. Embarrassed by her tears, she couldn't look at him. Arno scooped the back of her neck gently and drew her closer, pressed his forehead to hers. 'Kaya,' he said again, sincerely. 'I'm sorry.'

She swallowed as his jagged breathing slowed and soon she felt her heart rate matching his. Damn him, she couldn't even be mad at him for scaring her. Their chemistry got the better of them both, it seemed. She liked him so much.

'You were brave,' he told her, swiping a tear from her cheek with his good thumb.

'*You* could have been killed.'

'Not *"You were brave, too, Arno"*?' he teased.

Then he laughed softly and coughed again, and she sighed out her relief through her nose. He'd inhaled too much smoke, and his hand would bother him for a while, but he'd be fine.

He'd also gone out of his way to protect her, again, she thought helplessly as he searched her eyes, and scanned her lips in a way that made her heart ache and her throat even drier. He was everything she'd ever wanted; someone who'd always have her back, and her best interests at heart. The opposite of Pieter.

Standing up, she tore her eyes away, emotion trembling through her. They might not be indulging in any more overtly intimate moonlit moments, but he was the one she trusted, the only one she'd trusted fully in a long time—how could she not want him, when he acted like this?

What kind of mess had she landed herself in now?

The ambulance had rumbled off with their patients. Three firemen were hoisting bits of the mangled car onto a second truck already, and the hot sun beat down on her head, making her dizzy. She would likely have to drive them back herself, no thanks to his hand, or to the hospital, but she was thirsty and running out of energy fast.

The woman who'd been talking to Officer Marlo hurried over, taming back her wild dyed hair. Her vivid red dress was a beacon against the sky. 'I hear you saved that man's life,' she said to them, her hands running nervous trails along the chain of blue beads around her neck.

'We saw the explosion from the window. This is our property.'

Arno got slowly to his feet, accepting her help to steady him. Kaya gripped his arm; noting how his forearm took both of her hands to hold, and how the snake tattoo still seemed to taunt her, even covered in dirt. 'Yeah. Sorry about that, Mrs Wistuba,' he said, with another cough. 'I hope it didn't take out too much of the harvest.'

The woman frowned closer at Arno through her glasses, then her eyes widened in recognition. 'Arno Nkosi?' she cried in shock, pressing a hand to her mouth. 'Is that you? My goodness, does your mother know you're today's hero yet?'

CHAPTER THIRTEEN

KAYA WATCHED THE firemen remove the rest of the burnt-out car from her place on the front porch of Wistuba Winery's cellar door. She could barely make it out from this distance, but poor Mrs Nina Wistuba had been pouring her prize-winning Cabernet Sauvignon for the tourists behind closed doors when she smelled the smoke, then saw the explosion.

Arno drank a coffee in silence next to her, using his one good hand to grip the cup. Nina chattered into the phone by the steps, doing an interview with the local newspaper below several hanging baskets that were overflowing with the most magnificent shades of magenta and yellow Kaya had ever seen.

Nina, Arno's mother's closest friend, was refusing to let them leave until they'd rested a while longer, though it was obvious from his stance that Arno couldn't wait to get out of here.

'How's the hand now?' Kaya asked him softly, eager to break the silence.

'Fine.'

'You're not burdening me with anything by letting me help, you know, if that's what you're thinking,' she told him, realising he probably thought he'd just put her through enough—not that it was his fault! 'I'm going to have to check it later, in case you need stitches,' she added.

'You're welcome to, Doctor, but I won't.'

'How do you know that?'

'I know my own hands.'

'Why do you have to be so…?'

His phone chirruped like a cricket, and he fished around for it in three pockets before he found it, cursing at his hand while he did it. Kaya bit her tongue and studied the flowers, listened to him discuss the guy they'd pulled from the car, Daniel. His injuries were being treated in Cape Town. Thankfully it sounded as if he'd be OK, and he had his girlfriend with him. Maybe they'd think twice about driving tipsy or without their seat belts in future, she thought, disapprovingly. No wonder Arno was so against alcohol, if that was the kind of thing they saw regularly around here.

This tension between them was palpable. He was probably wishing he'd never kissed her and made things awkward. Already they were bickering.

No sooner had he hung up than his phone was ringing again.

'Popular,' she quipped.

Kaya saw *Mama Annika* flash up on the screen, but to her surprise he flipped his phone over and ignored it.

'You're not answering to your mother?' She couldn't keep the concern from her voice. 'She must have heard what happened, she's probably worried about you.'

'I'm alive, aren't I?' he said, crossing to the edge of the porch, away from her.

'Don't you think she'd like to hear that from you?' she said, but he merely shrugged, with his back to her. Damn him, shutting her out, and his mother, what was his problem? Kaya could almost see the weight on his shoulders as he rested his arms on the wooden railings and stared out across the vines.

Annoyed, she focused back on the hanging baskets, wishing she had her own phone with her. It would've been nice to send a message to her parents right about now. Something worse could have happened if she'd been just a couple of feet closer to that car when it exploded. And they worried about her, after everything she'd laid on them after the attack.

She'd been so distant after it, and living at home for three months afterwards hadn't helped her relationship with them...or with Pieter. Glancing at Arno, still staring at the vines, she wished she could see into his thick head. Why did she have to be falling for someone harder than she'd *ever* fallen for Pieter, especially someone she couldn't be with, especially out *here*, where she certainly did not belong?

Then again, where exactly did she belong? The more she thought about it, the less she knew. Going back home to her old job, working the night shift, where *she* was, the girl who'd seduced Pieter, wasn't a particularly encouraging thought.

Life was playing one big fat prank on her lately, throwing Arno into it like this.

'Now then, Kaya, how are you doing now? Have you had enough water? More tea?'

'I'm OK, thank you, Mrs Wistuba.' She smiled, gratefully. The kind Nina was done with her interview, hovering around the table, glancing between her and Arno. She lowered her voice. 'I hope that one's not giving you any trouble?'

'Who, Arno? Giving me trouble?' Kaya's stomach clenched. Maybe she'd heard their mild bickering—it certainly couldn't have looked professional.

Mrs Wistuba slid into the seat next to her, swiping at her brow. 'He can't much enjoy anything to do with cars going up in flames, not after what happened. But don't let his bad mood bring you down, it's nothing personal.'

'Oh, I know that,' Kaya said, flicking her gaze onto him, all hunched shoulders and sombre silence. Her heart went out to him suddenly. She'd been thinking about their personal…situation… but of course, he'd put himself in the line of fire again. 'I know about the fire at Nkosi Valley. All the people who died. It's awful, I saw the memorial.'

Nina Wistuba sat back in her chair, drumming her nails on the table. 'He showed you that?'

'Yes, when I stayed at his home.'

Nina was silent for a moment, seemingly trying to decipher her. 'Then you know it was all over the news,' she said. Her tone conveyed a fresh sadness that crept across the space between them into Kaya's bones. 'His poor mother. Losing her staff like that was bad enough, but when Annika lost the baby, nothing was quite the same for that family. I'm happy to see he's at least talking about it with someone now.'

Baby? Kaya blinked at her. 'Mama Annika lost a baby?'

Nina pulled a face, as if she'd accidentally revealed a secret. She lowered her voice even further, as perspiration tickled Kaya's neck. 'Are you two…together?'

'No, I'm a volunteer with the Lindiwe Foundation.'

'But he took you home? Annika says he never takes anyone home.'

Kaya kept her voice cool, even though her heart was a drum. 'Well, we had a run-in with an elephant and he had to run an errand there, after. So, there was a baby?'

Nina pursed her lips. Weirdly she didn't seem fazed about the elephant. 'Well, it's not really for me to say…but yes. Annika was pregnant when it happened. She was sleeping and she didn't wake up. Arno pulled her out. Annika was fine, but the baby… It was the smoke, they said.'

Kaya's hands found their way to her mouth. Her head was spinning.

So that was what Arno felt so bad about; what he'd failed to tell her. It was none of her business, and not his prerogative to tell her at all, but the pieces were falling together. He blamed himself for not being there. He thought it was unforgivable, going out, getting drunk, not being home when a pregnant Mama Annika needed him. His *older* pregnant mother, she realised now. He was only eighteen when it happened, twenty years ago.

Was he so caught up thinking it was all his fault that he never took anyone home in case they found out about it? He'd definitely seemed less than comfortable about her being there, that night. Couldn't get her away from his Mama fast enough. And he did say that before...that he felt as if people were judging him after the fire.

'What are you two gossiping about?' Arno broke into her thoughts, crossing the porch back to the table, eyes narrowed suspiciously. Kaya got to her feet before Nina could tell him what she assumed was something he wasn't too keen on sharing.

'We were just talking about...the flowers,' she said quickly, gesturing to the hanging baskets above the steps. 'I was just saying how I could do with some like this, for the garden.'

Thankfully, Mrs Wistuba seemed to read the room. Her beads swished as she stood, ushering them both from the porch into the barn, past the bar and barrels of wine and abandoned glasses, while Kaya wrestled with what to do about the barrel-load of new information she'd just received. If she told him she knew about Mama Annika and the baby, he might turn on her or stop talking to her altogether. He had to want to trust her and tell her himself.

'If you like those flowers, dear, wait till you see out the back,' Nina said, swinging open a huge, creaking wooden door at the back of the barn. 'I think you'll really like my sunflowers.'

* * *

Arno followed Nina Wistuba and Kaya through the garden he'd played in as a kid, with Nina's daughter, and vaguely heard them discussing different plants and flowers. His head was foggy, and his cough wasn't going away yet.

The eight-foot-high sunflowers towering over the pathways were impressive, and Kaya seemed excited to have seeds for her garden project, but he couldn't really concentrate on flowers right now. He felt bad for ignoring Mama Annika's call.

So bad.

But the last thing he needed was to have an emotional conversation with Mama in front of Kaya. She'd be upset, and rightly so, he might have been blown to pieces in a burning car. No doubt Nina had told her he was here, and what had happened on her property.

He was kind of torn up, if he was honest. The fire…the explosion. He'd put Kaya in a dangerous situation and now she was worrying *more* about his hand. Letting on that he was upset to Mama on top of all that—no. What right did he have to cause Mama any *more* concern?

Also, if he was totally honest with himself, he didn't want to be flung back to that day, when Mama's wailing could have taken down the hospital walls. He and Dad had had to bring her home to the charred house, all frail and broken; then Dad had gone off at him, telling him it had been his responsibility to look after her, to be there, to *protect* her. He'd never seen either of his parents cry before the miscarriage. *His* fault.

They never really spoke about it all. He tried not to, in case he ever saw the same blame in her eyes that he'd seen in his dad's, but maybe he *did* need to talk to her about it, for her sake.

Kaya had looked horrified just now, seeing him reject her call, and she was right to think him a selfish arsehole. She was right. Apart from Bea, Kaya was the only woman he'd ever let meet his mother; she'd seen the memorial too. She knew how the fire had affected them all... but she didn't know his brother died before getting the chance to live, because of him.

Watching the sunflowers arching over her ahead on the path, he felt suddenly compelled to tell this beautiful, honest woman the full extent of why he still found it so hard to be at home. Maybe he would if she wasn't going to be gone before her own sunflowers even blossomed in Mama Imka's village garden...

Arno stopped dead in his tracks.

Mama Imka.

Sunflowers.

'What's wrong? Is it your hand?' Kaya was at his side now, looking at him imploringly. Nina was halfway up the path, en route back to the house. Kaya took his hand and he let her study it, taking in every bit of her face, her mouth. Those predictions, whatever they were that Mama Imka had people so captivated by, weren't real.

'Arno? You've gone pale.'

This was a coincidence. Just a coincidence that they were standing here now in a garden full of sunflowers and she had him thinking things he'd never let himself think till now.

He realised he was staring at her, and he pulled his hand back quickly. 'I was just thinking I should go call Mama back,' he said. 'You're right, she's probably worried.'

Kaya's frown deepened. Her expression held the kind of perplexity that rattled his insides as the swaying sunflowers and their shadows seemed to mock him. 'Arno, I know we're not… talking about what happened,' she started. Impulsively he took her fingers in his, with his good hand.

'It was wrong of me to kiss you, and then act like it didn't happen,' he said.

'I did the same thing.'

'You don't let many people close to you, and neither do I. But that's no excuse, not after you told me what happened to you.'

Kaya smiled, shook her head at the grass. 'I don't think I knew what to do with it all either.'

'This is just all new to me,' he admitted. 'I don't usually do this with… I'm not sure what's right and what's wrong here.'

'Well—' she laced his fingers through her own '—I was just going to say that, even if nothing like that ever happens again, if you need someone to talk to about *anything*, I'm here. I'm your volunteer. I'm volunteering to hear you out.'

Arno rubbed at his chin, looking at their hands entwined, her slender fingers in his, the sweet tenderness in her eyes. The way she'd emphasised *anything* was almost as though she knew he held more demons inside him than he was willing to let escape. It didn't feel great, keeping such a big part of his story from her…but it would feel worse, seeing her react to the damage his selfishness had already done. He'd been through all that with Bea.

'Talk to me,' she said now. Her tone was nothing short of demanding. 'Did that car accident and the fire bring stuff back up for you? Is that why you didn't want to talk to your mother just now? It's OK to show a little emotion, you know, Arno, you'd be no less of a man for it. And you know by now, I'm a mess sometimes myself!'

'You make a mess out of me.' He groaned. She'd be gone before long; before her sunflowers got anywhere near this tall. Why tell her anything to help her change her mind about him now?

Kaya gasped softly as he swept her face closer with one hand. Her eyes fluttered shut and her lips looked so inviting he could hardly help sweeping a thumb from her cheek to her chin.

Maybe it was everything that had just happened, or the strange coincidence that had them standing here, having this conversation in the sunflowers, that got to him. It was quite possible that he didn't want to face *any* emotions right now in front of anyone, but kissing her again felt more right than wrong.

This time she didn't seem to want to stop at soft, light and tender. Her hands smoothed his cheeks and head, then brought his face forcefully forward, begging wordlessly for more from his lips as her hips crashed to his.

He loved the way her soft curls were bouncing around his face as they found themselves hidden from the house behind a tree. The warmth of her mouth rushed through to his heart, chasing away all the doubts, and he almost forgot how cold he'd felt this past week, telling himself he shouldn't do this again.

He was so caught up in the moment, and their mouths and lips and tongues, that he went to lay her down on the soft warm grass, where he could taste more of her, as much as she wanted him to taste. No one could see.

Kaya pulled away. His stomach plummeted as she sighed into her hands, then shot him a sheepish look that sent his hard-on right back to ground zero.

'I went too far with you.' He winced, scrambling back to standing.

'No, no, it's just…the grass, I don't know.' Kaya looked nervous now, leaning against the tree, touching her hair, looking up at the sunflowers, embarrassed. Arno could have kicked himself. This wasn't just any hungry, sex-obsessed woman who wanted him, this was someone who'd been taken advantage of and violated; he had to watch himself.

'It's not you,' she started, grimacing, hugging her arms around herself. 'I wanted you to kiss me, it's just…sorry.'

'I'm the one who should be sorry.' Arno was mortified for his behaviour, for the thoughts that had momentarily shoved his common sense aside.

'Not at all, Arno. This is so embarrassing.'

'Don't be embarrassed,' he told her, angry on her behalf now. What the hell did that guy do to her? He dared to reach for her, coaxing her slowly into an embrace, where hopefully she'd feel safe. She was so slender, so strong, but yet so fragile. Her bones felt like delicate branches he suddenly wanted to shield from every single storm. The need to protect her against all evils rose in him and coursed like fire through his veins. He was in out of his depth.

He wanted Kaya and wanted to be the one she turned to, at least while she was here, which meant he should probably tell her what had been eating at him since the day of that fire. She knew he was keeping something back; and she'd told him more than she probably ever meant to already, about herself.

This was it, he realised. Trust equalled trust. He had to trust she wouldn't turn away from him if she found out the truth about the pain he'd caused—the full reason he'd turned to medicine. Whatever happened from this point forward, and it would have to happen very, very slowly, if at all…all he wanted now was for her to trust him. If only it weren't so ingrained in him to keep all his emotions locked in a watertight box in the pit of his stomach.

CHAPTER FOURTEEN

KAYA RAN HER hands along Tande's coarse fur and closed her eyes. She was doing her best to project a sense of calm, although every time she met with the lioness it felt as if she were in the opening scene of a wildlife documentary before the brave and reckless tourist wound up as dinner.

'She likes you,' Arno whispered into her ear as Tande yawned, and stretched out on the ground next to them, her huge paws kicking up the dust.

'I hope so.' She sighed, resting her head back against his broad chest in the soft grass, feeling the first few rays of sunlight start to warm her skin. She'd forced herself to be OK with grass. After what had happened the other day in Mrs Wistuba's sunflower garden, when she'd made a fool of herself and ruined one of the best kisses of her life, she'd worked on it, sat outside amongst the birds and bees, sometimes alone. Sometimes with Arno and Tande, like this.

Grass didn't have to remind her of her faceless perpetrator, shoving her hard onto the damp ground and…ugh. No. Grass was good. Grass was hope, and peace and comfort, and a piece of the natural world she could love and trust again because of Arno. It was Tande's favourite thing, next to raw meat.

'Thank you for meeting me here, every morning this week,' Arno said now, dropping a lingering kiss to the side of her head that made her stomach perform a backflip and her coffee flask almost slip from her hands. Five-thirty a.m. had never been so good. It had become a routine, this past week or so. He'd kiss her goodnight at her door, in secret under the stars. She'd meet him again out here first thing in the morning to watch the sun rise with Tande. Then, they would go to the gym.

He liked to work out with his shirt off. Even with his bad hand he managed to lift weights with the other one, and every time she watched him grow a little bit stronger, a little bit more like the shield she never knew she'd been looking for, she got the kind of starry eyes that made her wonder if tonight would be the night he asked if he could stay in her room. Or ask if he could talk to her about what was really going on with him and his mother.

He never took her up on that listening ear. And he never asked if he could stay over.

If she wasn't trying her best to live in the moment for once, she'd be infuriated at all the things she still didn't know, and might never know, but she had to keep her head on straight.

'Are you coming with us on the outdoor expedition?' he asked her now, stroking a finger along her bare arm, and leaving a stray butterfly flapping around her heart.

The butterfly died suddenly at his question. She'd been wanting to go along on this weekend's trip, designed to introduce a group of school kids to survival tips and first aid in the wilderness, even though it was her weekend off, but Mark had signed up to go. So had Kimberley.

No one had said anything more about her and Arno since that night when Mark had grabbed her by the fire and got an earful from Arno in return. At least, not to their faces. But the last thing she needed was to be stuck in a tent with one of them, pretending things weren't totally awkward.

'Mark cancelled, he has to fly home for a birthday,' Arno told her, a sly smile on his lips. Was he reading her mind?

'Will I get my own tent?' she asked him as her heart sped up.

Silence.

She stroked her hand across Tande's back and waited for Arno to say she wouldn't need one, that they could share, but instead he nodded quietly, eyes narrowed. 'Everyone gets their own tent. We leave tonight after dinner.'

The whole day, on their rounds at two different villages, Kaya saw to her TB patients, administered treatment for a lung infection, and answered another barrage of questions about sex from teenagers at the school where they'd given their talk, all the while trying not to think of how torturous it would be this weekend, being so close to Arno without being able to touch him.

He'd watched like a hawk this afternoon, from the other side of the garden as she'd pressed the new sunflower seeds into the earth with the kids, as if he were worried she would fly away too soon. But he wasn't making any real moves beyond kissing, and she didn't quite know how to feel about that. If someone had told her just a couple of months ago that she'd be imagining herself in bed with a South African doctor, her mentor no less, she'd have laughed.

No, she wouldn't have laughed actually, she'd have been terrified. The thought of all that had been terrifying for so long; it felt strange to *want* to be touched. But he wasn't initiating anything. And it was probably best. The last thing she needed was for all those hormones to rush back in and render her attached to a man she had no business getting any more attached to.

Back at Thabisa, Kimberley poked her head around the door as she was packing for the camping expedition, in a red baseball cap to match her rosy cheeks.

'Got everything?'

'Yes, ma'am,' Kaya answered, grabbing a book she knew she'd bury herself in at nights, alone in her tent; anything to stop herself wanting to go to Arno.

'I'm glad you're coming,' Kimberley said, hovering in the doorway. 'Have you forgiven me yet, for what happened that night, when Mark… you know?'

Kaya sighed. She couldn't avoid this for ever. 'I hold no grudges against either of you. You were just asking me what's going on with Dr Nkosi. I suppose you have to work with us, and you're not blind.'

'So, there's an "us"?' Kimberley cocked one eyebrow, stepping further into her room. 'It will go no further, I promise. I kind of hoped there was. You two make a cute couple.'

Cute. Ugh. What a word.

Kaya huffed a laugh she didn't really feel. 'There's no "us",' she told her, carefully. 'But there's *something*, I guess.'

Kimberley dropped to her bed and eyed her, throwing a sweater and camo trousers into her bag with her toothbrush. 'What will you do when you have to go home?'

Kaya's heart lurched. Tears sprang to her eyes without warning and she bit down on her cheeks, pausing with her packing. Hearing it spoken out loud by someone else made the truth sink in. She wasn't staying here, she didn't belong. Arno's life existed on a whole different continent, and he couldn't exactly up sticks and move to the Netherlands with his lioness.

'Nothing,' she said, forcing her voice to stay neutral, turning away from Kimberley's intrusive gaze. 'I'll just keep living my life, like he will.'

Kimberley snorted indignantly. 'Listen to you,' she said, slapping a hand to her heart dramatically. 'God, girl, if I scored someone like *him*, I'd never let him go.'

'But...we live in totally opposite hemispheres!'

'So? Didn't you say something about your mama being from here, in one of our intro sessions? She moved to be with your dad, didn't she?'

Kaya's heart had started to go a little haywire. She sank to the bed next to Kimberley, suddenly grateful the brash Australian had reached out with a new perspective on her whirring inner monologues. Yes, her mother crossed the world to be with her dad after their whirlwind romance, but that was then, and they were different.

Kimberley chatted at her while she finished packing, and she did her best to focus, and not to let herself think along those lines about herself and Arno—he didn't want to start some relationship with her, surely. He couldn't even open up to her about his past after she'd given him the chance. He didn't *want* to get that close.

It was a tender, loving, intimate, temporary thing that was helping her self-confidence, and making his days less lonesome, that was all.

'You don't have much time left to snare him.' Kimberley grinned.

'I'm not trying to snare him!'

'Well, maybe you should.'

Kaya crinkled up her nose—there was nothing worse than being put on the spot like this. But maybe she *was* looking for excuses not to get that close herself. This was everything she'd felt for Pieter at the start multiplied by a million. Being cheated on had left some kind of nasty scar around her heart, and if anyone else ever did that…if Arno ever did that, or even just called it off, the pain of it all might just kill her.

The questions from the kids were flooding in as usual. Arno usually loved this part of the first night of camp, when everything was fresh and exciting. They were sitting around the fire under the moonlight on the disused logging trail behind the Berg River Dam, listening to the croaking frogs.

He'd started a discussion about plastic bags and their choking effects on small streams, how they smothered the larvae of unborn frogs and cut off their sun and air. Kaya was listening to everything intently, scribbling in her notebook as much as the kids, and he was glad she was here, even if she wasn't pleased with him.

Not pleased at all.

She'd seen him ignore another call from Mama Annika, right before boarding the bus from Thabisa. She asked him why he'd done that, again. He told her he would text Mama Annika, that he needed to talk to her face to face in private, and clearly, Kaya felt excluded. She reminded him that they were going off grid into the wilderness with no reception, but still he'd shrugged it off, like a selfish idiot, and refused to explain why the need for privacy—they were too close for secrets now, and his was eating him up but it was something he needed to face alone.

'Can we go for a night swim?' one of the girls was asking now.

He was about to answer the girl with a resounding 'No, not tonight' when she turned to Kaya and asked her the same question.

'I don't think that's the plan for tonight, right, Arno?' she said tactfully, casting her eyes at him for confirmation.

The girl pouted, her friends jeered *boo*, while Arno replied, 'Right.' But he held Kaya's eyes like glue. It was the first thing she'd really said to him since arriving.

A moment passed.

Then she tore her eyes away, leaving him cold.

'Let's discuss the critters, shall we?' he said, squaring his shoulders, inviting more questions. They all wanted to know about the spiders and usually he loved to enlighten them on identification, habitat, and first-aid treatment of their various bites and stings.

Now, though, Kaya's eyes held the sting of a thousand scorpions. He still owed her an explanation as to why things were so tense with Mama Annika; she was probably more insulted that he was clearly keeping something from her when she'd opened up to him about her own issues... which were worse, and way more recent.

He'd almost told her several times. All those mornings she'd sat with him watching the sun rise over the mountains with Tande this past week, he could have just told her then, put his trust in her, as she'd put her trust in him.

But what if she pulled away from him, as Bea had?

Coward!

OK, yes, he was a coward. He liked her too much, already. It should probably stop—this thing, whatever it was turning into—but, just as selfishly, he didn't want it to.

'What's the most venomous spider out here?' Kaya was asking now. He shoved his hands into his pockets, wondering why such an innocent question seemed so loaded.

'That would be the six-eyed crab spider,' he said. 'They might be the most venomous spiders in the world, but they're pretty solitary and secretive creatures.'

'Oh, yes. I know those kinds of creatures,' she said thoughtfully. 'Solitary. Secretive…'

Arno cleared his throat, ignored a smirk from Kimberley and moved the subject matter on to the first aid. 'You'll be learning some really essential life-saving techniques this weekend, starting tomorrow. How to care for a sprained ankle, how to stop a bleeding nose, what to do and what not to do with a fractured limb…'

Kaya was unnerving him. Talking to a group wasn't as easy as it usually was and he recognised his guilt again, plaguing him as it had for years every second he lost focus.

He'd called Mama Annika several times since they'd pulled the tourist from the car wreck; more than usual, in fact, which was kind of nice after all this time. She definitely appreciated hearing from her son more often, and talking about her art. Likewise, he liked to hear it.

Only now she was asking for him to go visit again, and to bring Kaya—Nina Wistuba must have mentioned something about them coming back to the porch a *long* time after she'd left them in her garden—and he was stalling.

He'd already decided to face her about the fire, thanks to Kaya, really. She'd got him thinking, without really knowing the full extent of what he'd done. It *was* time they talked it out, time he admitted Dad was right that night, he should've protected her and his soon-to-be brother, time he heard it from her too and apologised and maybe even tried to put it behind them.

But whenever he decided to do it, he backed out. Things were good right now. Shouldn't he just enjoy the time he had left with Kaya? He wasn't ready to break down the past just yet.

Excuses.

Kaya stuck her hand up again. 'What do I do if my tent won't stay up?'

'What?'

She gestured with a finger to where he'd helped her put the tent up, just thirty minutes ago. Sure enough, Kaya's tent had doubled in on itself and was inexplicably crumbled in a heap of useless canvas on the groundsheet.

Arno stormed across to it, inspecting the material while the kids broke into laughter and chatter behind them. Kaya was at his side now.

'I don't get it,' he said, dashing a hand across his head in confusion. This had never happened before. These were military grade tents and he'd been using them for years with no issues. Maybe it had been on its last legs on the last trip, when they'd suffered through that mountaintop gale, and he hadn't noticed.

'I can't sleep in this. It's broken,' she mused. 'Maybe some*thing* has broken it.'

Her eyes grew round in fear.

'What if it was a lion, or a cheetah?'

'Cats around here don't attack tents, they're not even in this national park,' he said. He'd never bring this group somewhere that unsafe, or Kaya, for that matter. The look she gave him, all big, beguiling eyes, struck his core like a thunderbolt. He wouldn't be *that* guy.

'You can sleep in Kimberley's tent,' he told her, before he could invite her into his. 'Not mine.'

'I wasn't suggesting I sleep in *yours*,' she shot back haughtily, dropping his arm and grappling for her sleeping bag amongst the canvas, but he didn't miss the hurt in her eyes.

He pulled out her backpack and crossed to Kimberley's tent with it. Kaya followed and tossed her sleeping bag through the doorway, heavily.

Zipping the tent up roughly, he felt her eyes lasering his back, and when he stood, she was right there, arms crossed, an inch from his lips, almost daring him to change his mind. He resisted the impulse to reach for her waist in the shadows, and strode back to the group, picked up his spider talk.

All night around the fire, he kept on catching her eye, searching for a sign that she wasn't mad at him. Oh, man, she was mad at him. Maybe even more annoyed than before, but he would not be swayed, not on this matter.

Of course, he wanted her in his damn tent, but they were out here *working* and, besides, he wasn't about to put either of them in that situation. She wasn't ready for what he'd want to do with her so close, even if she thought she was, and he wasn't going to be the one to initiate anything, not after what had happened the last time he'd got careless and let his impulses override his chivalry.

It wasn't all about his refusal to get physical anyway. Something else was keeping him away. Their work here was dangerous. There were fires, and storms and guns and animals and other bad people out there... She was one brave woman, considering what she'd endured, but he couldn't always be there to protect her, even if he wanted to be. Bea might've thought he'd let her down eventually, one way or another, and left before he got the chance. Kaya could do that too.

OK, so he couldn't predict the future, but he could start by not putting her in danger of *him*.

CHAPTER FIFTEEN

KAYA YAWNED, HER SLEEPINESS causing her to stumble on the hiking trail. Sweeping the branches out of her face, she tried to stay focused on the young boy from Johannesburg she was walking beside, who was telling her about practising first aid on his dog, but all she wanted to do was slump in a heap on the ground.

Kimberley had snored the entire night in her ears. She'd lain awake in the deplorable volume of it, wishing she could just be braver and go to Arno's tent instead. But he didn't want her there; he didn't even want to *talk* to her about anything real, like the reason he found it tough to be around Mama Annika.

That ignored phone call had played on her mind all night, too. The fact that for whatever reason he didn't want her to know the full story about the night of the fire was almost worse than it would've been, not knowing anything herself. He was holding back on talking, on trying to take things further, because she was difficult to be around—obviously—and because this thing was getting out of hand. She was leaving, *soon*. His reticence was totally understandable. He didn't want to invest emotionally *or* physically. Neither should she.

Last night, in the maddening vibration of Kimberley's snoring, she'd decided to call it off with him. No more sunset meet-ups, no more kisses. It was all just getting too weird and complicated. Her heart wasn't designed to handle this!

If only he didn't look so damn hot out here, out of his uniform T-shirts, leading this group on the trail along the dam and into the bush, like an expert commander in his hiking boots, all muscles in his sleeveless shirt.

Groan.

Damn him, sending her heart into a fluttering mess every time she tried to be mad at him. She should tell him. *I want this thing between us to be over.* But she couldn't seem to find the words to tell him something she didn't quite mean.

Soon, it was lunch time, and he caught her while the kids were chattering noisily over pre-packed boxes of chicken and rice by the river. The sky was dotted with fluffy white clouds, just a hint of grey she hoped wouldn't turn to rain later.

'How was last night?' he asked her, handing her a coffee. She must have looked as if she needed it.

'Great, if you like sleeping next to a chainsaw,' she told him, and his mouth twitched.

'I thought you looked tired. I can give you some earplugs for tonight if you like.'

Kaya scowled over the coffee cup, wishing she weren't so drawn into his twinkling eyes, and enchanted by the shape of his way too kissable mouth. This would be the perfect time to tell him what she'd decided last night—that when they got back to Thabisa there would be no more making out, no more cosy gym sessions or sunrises, but she couldn't do it.

'No earplugs?' he said now, running his eyes over her lips in a way that turned her bare knees to jelly. He reached a hand to her hair and swept it behind her ear, and for a second his eyes seemed to glaze over, before he remembered where they were. He pulled his hand back, leaving her heart racing.

'I'll get them from you later,' she told him, putting her cup down, flustered. 'Don't worry, I won't come into your tent.'

He muttered something under his breath, stepping closer, then he ushered her quickly away from the group, down to the reeds along the riverbank.

'You know why you can't stay in my tent, don't you?' he said, cupping her face in his hands.

Her heart leapt to her throat as the reeds tickled the skin around her shorts. The frogs were so loud, messing with her head. His gaze was all intensity, threatening to unravel her resolve.

'Not just because we're working, and the kids are here, and—'

'Listen,' she said, cutting him off before she chickened out again. 'You don't want to take things any further with me. I understand, Arno. I probably freaked you out last time we tried...'

Arno's eyebrows shot to the sky. 'You think I don't *want* to take things further?'

'I'm a difficult person to get close to.' She lowered her voice, shook her head, trying not to be swayed by his closeness or her attraction to him, which was flying through the roof just being in his hands.

'But so are you, Arno. You don't trust me.'

He frowned. 'What do you mean?'

'It doesn't matter now. You don't want me to get close to you, and I get it, I do. I'm leaving. This should all probably stop, Arno, it won't end well. It's too much for me.'

Arno searched her eyes and she saw helplessness, desperation, before it was shuttered out by the usual stubbornness. His lips drew into a thin line.

'If it's too much for you, then yes, we stop. Now.'

She felt sick, suddenly. Was that the only part he'd heard?

Kaya forced herself not to reach for him as he stood with her. She felt like saying that wasn't *exactly* what she'd meant…the physical stuff didn't feel like too much, but the thought of having it, and loving it, then losing it was definitely too much. Pieter flashed into her mind—as he always did at the worst of times, but now she was starting to see the situation differently. He'd backed into Claudette's arms, but only because she had pushed him there by hating herself too much to let him touch her. She'd felt dirty, as though a part of her were always unclean, and only now was she starting to feel whole again, and worthy—because of Arno!

But she couldn't quite articulate all that, and he was already pulling away. She could literally feel him letting her go.

It was better this way, she told herself. This was a whole different situation; she could hurt even worse, way, way worse if she fell for this one and couldn't make it work. Her parents made it work, the voice in her head yelled, but that was their story, not hers. Aside from everything else her whole life was in Europe, and this man's most definitely was not. The Band-Aid way was the only way. Get it over with fast so it wouldn't hurt.

By late afternoon, the kids had practised how to do basic life-saving mouth-to-mouth breathing and cardiac massage. Arno had patiently demonstrated how to feel for a pulse, to listen and to look for signs of breathing, and also how to alleviate the excruciating stings and bite wounds left by various creatures in the wild.

It was excruciating being out here, knowing she'd never touch Arno or kiss him again. Every time she met his eyes, adrenaline pumped like petrol through her veins, making her dizzy. Was she too hasty earlier, pushing him away? Was she just annoyed over his secrecy, scared that he was pushing her away first? This was all so confusing.

Nothing had ever been so confusing in her life. Kimberley kept asking what was wrong. 'I'm just tired,' she told her.

'Was I snoring?'

'A little,' she replied tactfully, but poor Kimberley looked embarrassed, which made her feel even worse about the day.

Somehow Kaya took over the part of the session at camp where she explained the mantra of good first aid: *First do no harm...you'll be more help if you just stay calm.*

She was just about to explain the many ways in which a helper in a hysterical mindset could lead to an even bigger injury when the little boy—Stefan—she'd been talking to on the hike about his dog, called out to her.

'Kaya!'

She frowned, noticing his suddenly pale face.

'My hand hurts.'

She exchanged a glance with Arno, just before the boy started screaming and clutching his arm. 'Now my whole arm hurts!' he yelped, before hunching over on the ground.

For a second, everyone froze and stared. Except herself and Arno.

'What's the matter?' she demanded, rushing over, taking his head onto her lap on the grass, while Arno raced for medical supplies. Stefan could barely keep his eyes open now and was clutching his arm to his chest as if he were worried it might fall off.

'It's some kind of allergic reaction,' Arno said, back at her side, checking the boy's eyes with a torch. In the background Kimberley was ushering the remaining panicking kids away to the riverbank, where they couldn't watch and be frightened. Then, Kaya saw the size of Stefan's hand. It was swollen so much now it was almost twice the size as normal.

'Arno, look!'

Arno's eyes narrowed next to her as she cradled Stefan's head. Together they inspected the bizarre but telling black dot, circled with a white ring on the back of the boy's right hand. 'Spider bite,' he said gravely. Stefan was frothing at the mouth now, slurring his speech as he tried to complain. 'Shh,' she soothed. 'We're going to help you…you'll be OK.'

She lowered her voice. 'It's not the six-eyed crab spider, is it?' she said, watching Arno fish around in the bag for a syringe. The boy was struggling to breathe already and seemed to be slipping into some sort of fever dream in her arms.

'I don't know. I don't think so, it looks like a black widow bite.'

'Black widow?' Kaya's mind reeled as she held Stefan closer, protectively. 'That's almost as bad, isn't it?'

'Not quite, we caught it just in time.'

The boy was sweating but felt cold and clammy to the touch. Arno pulled the cap off a bottle of liquid and told her to hold him still. In less than twenty seconds he'd administered the full vial of antivenom, and Kaya realised she was trembling with adrenaline, sitting on the muddy floor. Were there other spiders here, ready to issue venomous bites to everyone else? How on earth had they missed this?

'Stefan didn't say anything about his hand till just now. It must have all happened so fast!' she said out loud. She bit her tongue as Arno met her eyes, remembering the talk she had literally just given the kids on staying calm.

She was the opposite of calm, suddenly. Was she to blame here? She'd been too distracted by Arno, all afternoon, torn over her decision to call things off, to notice *anything*.

'I should have seen this sooner.'

Arno must have seen the look on her face. He put a hand to her arm gently. 'There was nothing to see, it came on so fast. It's no one's fault. He's already getting colour back in his cheeks, look.'

'Arno,' she whispered, cradling the boy even closer. 'People can die from black widow bites.'

He nodded, packing up the syringe in its wrapper. 'Small children, people who are already sick, and very old people, maybe, but he's fine, this antivenom works at short notice, don't worry.'

'You've seen this before?' Kaya couldn't keep the shock from her voice.

'Of course, I have. This isn't Amsterdam.' With that, he snapped the bag shut, motioned to her to follow him with it, and took the boy gently from her arms. Stefan was coughing and clasping his arm, which thankfully was already decidedly less swollen. 'He'll need half an hour or so for the drugs to take full effect. We'll dress the wound on his hand with antibiotic cream. He'll be OK.'

She followed as he carried the boy to his tent. *This isn't Amsterdam.* Did he really just have to highlight how they were from two different planets? The most dangerous things in Amsterdam were the trams and the cyclists…and weird, stoned, drunk men in parks at night, she thought with a chill. She was out of her league here, way out of her league and of course he knew it. Sure, there were moments when she dared to think she had this life all worked out, mostly gazing at some romantic sunrise, but she'd barely scratched the surface of Arno's world and she was way too green, at the end of the day, to ever live somewhere like this for ever. The thought left a dull ache in the pit of her stomach.

She helped him apply the cream and wrapped Stefan's hand with a gauze while Arno checked his blood pressure. 'He's fine, he'll sleep it off. If he wants to go home later, I'll take him.'

'I don't want to go home!' the boy mumbled groggily, and Arno huffed a laugh.

'Tough guy, huh?'

'Need me to watch him a while?' she asked.

Arno got to his haunches. 'I'll stay with him for now. Go tell the others he's OK, we handled it.'

She sighed and slunk back outside, feeling helpless and searching the ground at her feet for spiders. Always some different new drama out here; it really wasn't Amsterdam. Home would be considerably less interesting after all this.

Arno's pride had probably taken a kicking, hearing her call things off as she had done; she hardly expected things between them to be fine straight away, but till now she hadn't really considered what a culture shock it would be, going *home* after this.

She could learn something new every day if she stayed longer, carried on working with Arno...maybe there was some kind of future, like Mum and Dad had made happen for themselves. They could always visit, if she stayed on. They'd love visiting here more often, spending time with all the animals, and the kids. Mum would love Tande, she thought dreamily, before kicking herself.

Ugh. What was she even *thinking?* She must be delirious—definitely needy—after years of thinking she could never need anyone like this, also scared he'd go cold on her from now on when she was here to grow a backbone—alone.

The rest of the night, while poor Stefan rested

and she, Arno and Kimberley took turns to monitor him, her head continued to hurricane around the notion of actually ending this volunteer position, or extending it, maybe with another foundation or facility.

It wasn't just about Arno! She might be too old for her parents' concern by most people's standards, but they knew what she'd been through. Mum had said more than once in her emails how dangerous it could be here, if she stepped foot in the wrong direction at the wrong time. Come home soon...stay safe out there...don't do anything silly... All the things a worried mother could say were right there in her emails. A million different ways to say they missed her.

God knew she'd put them both through enough after the attack. It wasn't fair that they'd still be worrying about her every day out here. There was also work. The hospital had offered her a new position, no more night shifts with Claudette. She was over that anyway. Claudette was welcome to Pieter; even if she did see her at the hospital, she was *much* stronger now, with or without Arno!

She jutted her jaw out, clenched her teeth.

OK, so it wasn't ideal. But it was *something*, till she figured out what was next. She could do a lot now she'd finally got her backbone back! This place had been good for her but home was calling. She'd done the right thing distancing herself from potential heartbreak, she told herself resolutely, glancing at the greying sky just as the thunder rumbled ominously from the mountains.

'Looks like we might get some rain tonight, guys,' Arno told the group, prodding at the embers of a dying fire. 'Make sure you zip your tents up properly.'

He threw her a lingering gaze that crept deep into her bones and probed at her soul. His eyes spoke volumes about wanting her, despite all the weirdness between them. For a split second she forgot she'd called things off. A flashback struck, him kissing her in that sunflower garden; the softness of his lips on hers, then hard and hungry, the start of something new. She'd fallen for him irrevocably then, and she could have sworn he felt the same.

If her ex's kisses had been ice cream and honeycomb and all the candies she could've wanted, Arno's were strengthening pulses and nourishing juices and all the things she *needed*. He filled her up and left her satisfied. The most incredible kisses of her entire life so far had been with him. Oh, to have one more kiss with him like that, and *feel* like that, and not ruin it next time.

She groaned to herself, breaking his gaze. There couldn't be a next time! What was the matter with her? Had she not just decided?

Better for her to go to bed.

She was so exhausted, so tired of trying to figure out what was right, and what was wrong. But all she wanted, she realised, was to lie down and sleep for a week in the arms of the man she'd pushed away.

CHAPTER SIXTEEN

ARNO SMACKED A fist to his pillow, trying to get it just right. Damn camping pillows were always too small, they never fitted his head right. Not that he would've been able to sleep; the rain was almost deafening and Kaya was refusing to get out of his head.

'It won't end well. It's too much for me.'

Just those words had felt like a bullet to his chest. He'd pushed her too far; with the early morning meet-ups and kisses and caresses. They were verging on becoming a couple, sex or no sex, which was never going to end well for either of them. Volunteers never stayed long.

But that wasn't the real issue here.

He pummelled the pillow again as the thunder rumbled outside, brought it down over his head and growled into it, deep, guttural. She thought he didn't trust her. That was the killer. Was it that obvious he was holding back? He should've told Kaya when he had the chance, trusted her, let her in.

'Arno, are you awake?'

He threw the pillow aside. 'Kaya?' She was standing outside his tent in the rain—was she crazy? Quickly he won the fight with the zip at the door and she stepped inside in a pair of night shorts and a vest top, brushing the rain from her bare arms.

'Sorry... I couldn't sleep again. I came to get the earplugs.'

He stared at her from the warmth of his sleeping bag as she dropped to her knees. His brain wasn't quite registering she was actually here.

'Right, of course, I have some...' Rummaging through his backpack, he became aware of her breathing, short, sharp, as if she was nervous. The small tent shrank around them and the frogs outside intensified their rain song. Where were the damn earplugs?

'Sorry if I woke you,' she said now, sniffing against the cold.

'You didn't, I couldn't sleep,' he admitted. His fingers closed around the tiny plastic box and he clasped it in his palm as the rain on the canvas quickened in fury, a thousand hands pummelling the canvas. She said nothing but her teeth were chattering. He zipped up the open door behind them quickly, grabbed the extra sleeping bag, wrapped it around her shoulders tightly, then handed her the earplugs.

'Wait a minute at least. You'll be soaked if you go out now,' he said, resisting the urge to wipe a raindrop from her eyelashes. She sucked in a breath, an inch from his lips. He'd never seen her in sleep shorts, all tiny and fragile and sleepy, and suddenly he wanted to draw her close, nuzzle up to the warmth of her and have her protect *him* from his own incessant thoughts, and tell her…everything.

'What did you mean when you said I don't trust you?' he started.

Kaya frowned into the sleeping bag as she brought it up to her chin. She sighed through her nose. 'I know Mama Annika had a miscarriage after the fire, Arno. I know about the baby who died.'

What?

Arno sat cross-legged his sleeping bag, facing her with his heart in his throat. So much for finally telling her himself. 'How did you…?'

'Nina told me. She thought I knew about it. I know you feel bad about that. You think Mama Annika blames you, and that's probably why you're not as close to her as you could be, right? Why you ignore her calls?'

'She said that?'

'Not all of it, no, I figured it out, from the way you are.'

Arno was speechless. He ran a hand over his jaw, thrown. She'd known all this time? Not just what happened, but she'd figured out the guilt that followed him around, strapped to his ankles like leaden chains. He didn't know whether to be angry, or relieved, or impressed…what was this feeling?

'I gave you the chance to talk to me about it,' she said now. 'Stupidly I thought maybe I'd be the one to make you realise you shouldn't feel guilty about anything. You were eighteen, you were just living your life, how were you to know a fire would break out? But I don't think you wanted to tell me anything at all, did you?'

He balled his fists around the sleeping bag, let the rain fill in the silence. This was not how he'd expected this to go. 'I didn't want you to look at me differently,' he tried to explain. 'It's my fault I wasn't there to get her out, Kaya. I know that. My brother died because of me. It's not exactly something I'm going to shout from the rooftops when I *like* someone.'

Kaya's eyes shone fiercely in the slip of moonlight creeping through the tiny mesh window.

'No one died because of you, Arno. They died because there was a *fire*.'

'That's not what my father thinks,' he said.

She blinked. 'What do you mean?'

'He blames me. When we got back from the hospital with Mama, he told me I should have been there to protect her, and he was right.'

'Those are two different things, Arno! When did he actually say he blames you for Mama losing the baby?'

Arno paused, reliving the conversation from all those years ago in his head. They'd both been emotional, his dad especially. He'd almost lost the love of his life. Looking at Kaya, Arno could see it all now, from his father's perspective.

'I'd bet my life he doesn't blame you,' Kaya said. 'You just decided that the miscarriage was your fault and took on all the shame. The same way I told myself Pieter ditched me because I wouldn't sleep with him. You made me see this, Arno, the way you've been so good and patient with me, even knowing *everything* about what happened! Pieter dumped me because I let the shame of it all ruin the way I looked at myself. I turned into someone else, someone even *I* couldn't stand, and for what purpose?'

Her voice was wobbling now, almost setting him off as he shuffled closer impulsively, wrapped his arms around her. 'I mean, how did that serve me, Arno? He cheated on me, with one of my friends!'

The emotion in her voice now was unbearable. He held her closer, tighter, and she sank against him. 'I don't want to be someone who can't be touched,' she continued, pressing her face to his heart. 'I don't want *you* to look at *me* differently, like Pieter did. I want you to trust me and talk to me and make love to me…' She trailed off, blew air through her nostrils. 'Because you're amazing. You shouldn't feel guilty about anything, you did what you could at the time and look at everything you're doing now. You're…amazing.'

'Kaya…'

'But at the same time, I don't want you to trust me and talk to me, and make love to me, because I don't belong here. Soon I'll never see you…'

'Is that why you called things off?' He choked into the top of her soft head. He realised he was willing his own voice not to tremble now; he wasn't used to all this emotion. It was exactly what he'd swallowed back all these years in case a tidal wave of it consumed him. But he'd severely misinterpreted what Kaya was going through. Even letting him get this close to her was a bigger deal to her than he'd ever imagined, and he'd paid her back by insulting her intelligence.

Kaya pushed him off her and scrambled out of the sleeping bag, swiping at her eyes. Arno's vision was blurry; what the hell just happened? 'Baby, what are you doing?'

She was tugging at the zip on the door now, desperate to get out. He scrambled after her. 'Kaya, stop!'

'Thank you for the earplugs,' she said, finally managing to dislodge the zip. She almost tripped on her way out, leaving her boots behind in the doorway, and Arno followed her barefoot into the rain, cursing that he couldn't call for her in case he woke everyone up.

He caught her halfway to Kimberley's tent, took her hips, swung her around. Her hair dripped rain into her eyes that slid from her eyelashes as she gasped in surprise.

'Is that why you called things off?' he said again, scooping her face closer. 'Because you think once you're done with this position, I'll never want to see you again?'

She shook her head, flattening her palms to his bare chest as the thunder cracked above them. 'It's impossible.'

Arno's stomach clenched. Maybe she was right, but he couldn't bring himself to imagine never wanting to see her again, not even if she *was* on the opposite side of the planet. She knew everything about him now, and she still wanted to see him, still worried deeply about losing him. It had been for ever since anyone had known the real him, maybe no one ever had, and Kaya wanted him anyway.

He lifted her chin, pressed his lips to hers and kissed her, to hell with the rain, and impossibilities. She responded with heat and hands and passion that made the knots inside him unravel. 'Whatever happens, I'm here for you,' he said. 'Would I kiss you like this if I wasn't? Would I even be here?'

He gestured to the rain and she shook out her arms, then looped them back around his shoulders, half laughing with the cold and emotion. 'I didn't mean to give you any reason to think I'd keep things from you… It's just, twenty years of carrying that around, it's not so easy to talk about it with anyone.'

'I see you,' she said, and she kissed him again, and again, crashing her tongue to his in the rain, till they were staggering back to his tent, falling through the door, arms and legs a wet, tangled mess on top of the sleeping bags.

The tent didn't feel too small any more as they kissed, and kissed, and wrapped their bodies around each other. It felt right to Kaya, like their own protective bubble. She was drenched, just like Arno, but the cold couldn't reach her here.

Straddling him on the sleeping bag, she leaned over him, pressed her mouth to his again, soaking in the hot deliciousness of his kisses. To hell with her fears getting in the way. No one had ever made her feel like this.

He groaned softly beneath her and she felt his hardness through her shorts. Thrilled, she wondered how this had happened so fast; she'd broken things off, but he wasn't going anywhere. Arno wanted her, even though she'd dredged his deepest darkest secret out into the open. He still felt guilty, she knew that much, but he wouldn't for ever, not if she could help it.

She slid her languid palms along his torso, along his arms, around his navel, memorising the feel of his flesh against hers, committing his contours to memory in the half-light. His hands came up in her hair and she arched her back, then slid her vest top up over her head.

Arno stilled beneath her. She felt the rise and fall of his chest between her thighs, the heady thrum of his heartbeat, same as hers. Taking his hands, she covered them with hers and traced them up over her stomach, stopping just below her breasts.

Drawing a slow, deep breath, she closed her eyes and continued inching his hands, in hers, up slowly over her naked breasts, where she paused, waiting…waiting for what?

The fear and nausea never came; the panic refused to find her. Desire flooded her belly as she pressed his hands to her breasts, wondering at the feel of them, big, warm, protective, cupping all of her, as if his hands were built to hold her.

He slid them back down her stomach, over her hips, up and down her spine slowly in wonder, exploring the feel of her skin tentatively as she rocked atop him, marvelling at the feel of his hardness against her shorts, all for her. Something to love, not to be afraid of, something that would never hurt her.

'Will you please make love to me?' The words left her mouth without a thought. Lowering her mouth to his, letting her hand slide down to the band of his shorts, she trembled in anticipation as she went to reach for him. She was ready to touch him; ready to be touched. Finally, here was everything she'd ever wanted.

With a frustrated sound, Arno clasped her hand, then removed it.

'No, Kaya,' he said, bringing her fingers to his mouth instead.

'I *want* you to. I'm saying it's OK.'

'I said no, not here.' Arno sat upright, lifted her easily from astride him and laid her down gently onto her back, arching over her.

She froze beneath him. His face was obscured by the shadows, a faceless force, and she gasped for breath, scrambling up and away from him, covering her face in her hands as fresh mortification consumed her.

Breathe, breathe, breathe... It's Arno. It's not him!

'I'm sorry,' she cried, devastated. 'It's not you...'

'I know, it's OK, calm down.'

'I was fine, when I was in control, when I was on top...'

'This is why I'm not doing it,' he said gruffly, reaching for something in the dark. To her horror he pulled on a shirt, rummaged around for something else, and in a second he was shining a torch up at the roof. He held out his hand, eyes narrowed in compassion, and just the tiniest bit of annoyance—at himself, no doubt—and there was the nausea, swirling through her stomach, chasing all the butterflies out. She'd done it again. Proven she was broken.

'You're not ready,' he said to her softly, kindly, still holding his hand out to her. 'It's OK, Kaya, you can't rush it and I won't let you.'

But we don't have time not to rush, she felt like saying, but she couldn't even muster any words.

She took his outstretched hand in the torchlight, and he helped her into a sleeping bag, snuggled up close to her in his own, draped an arm around her. Moving into his big protective spoon, she tried not to blame herself. How could she?

Besides, he understood, he knew everything, and he was there for her…

This was *exactly* why she was falling for him, she thought in dismay as his breath ruffled her hair. This was why this would only hurt her more when it was over. It hadn't gone to plan today at all, ending things for good with Arno.

What exactly was she supposed to do, now?

CHAPTER SEVENTEEN

THE DAY DAWNED bright on the last morning of the expedition, and Kaya left his tent before sunrise, quietly, so no one at camp would be any the wiser. He heard the zip of Kimberley's tent, then he heard her start the fire, the clang of the pot for their coffee. He lay there alone for a few minutes, studying the canvas ceiling, gathering himself together.

Her sweet scent was all over his pillow.

Whatever had happened last night had thrown him all out of whack, but he had a bush survival skills class to teach before it was time to pack up and head to Thabisa, and he had to pull himself together.

Pulling on his clothes, he could still taste Kaya, still recall every inch of herself she'd revealed to him...the curves of her breasts in his hands, the look on her face when he'd told her no. The hardest damned thing he'd ever done!

He tore the zip up roughly, stepping into the

sunshine. She handed him a tin cup of steaming coffee.

Lucky that he did say no last night, he thought, eyeing her profile in the morning light against the backdrop of glistening wet leaves and craggy mountains. *Beautiful,* he thought. Mama Annika would love to paint her, just like this, if she had the chance.

'How are you feeling?' he asked her.

'I don't know,' she admitted, but she hid a small smile in her hair, and his lips curled in response as he clocked her still flushed cheeks, her swollen lips.

'You were a gentleman,' she said next, quietly. He wasn't sure if that reassured her or provoked the same deep agonising urges in her as it did him, even now, but they sank to the camping chairs and drank in silence in the ring of tents, tapping their boots against each other's.

He'd been right, she wasn't ready for more; not in the way she wanted to be. It only lit a fire in him, to be a better man for her. That Pieter guy cheated on her? After what she'd been through? The thought of it made his blood boil. No wonder she found it hard to let people close.

However long he had her for, he could still strive harder to be the kind of amazing she thought he was...which, of course, he wasn't.

Not to Mama anyway. Not yet, but he would change that. No more cowardly avoidance.

She turned to him suddenly. 'Arno, we should probably talk about—'

'Kaya?' Their spider-bite survivor, Stefan, was stepping out of his tent now, yawning sleepily. She shot Arno an apologetic look as she put her cup down and rushed to Stefan, got to her knees and checked his hand.

It was back to normal, as Arno knew it would be, and the kid still insisted he wanted to stick it out for their final day. Kids round here were brave; they had to be. Sometimes he wondered if his volunteers had seen half the strength from kids where they came from, as they saw out here.

Kaya was brave last night, too, he thought. He watched her while they set up the cereal station for breakfast, wishing he could go back to last night and stop himself sooner, before she'd even got the chance to try and give herself to him like that… What was he even doing, letting it go that far?

He'd got carried away, he supposed.

She probably just wanted to tell him it had to go slower, but she didn't need to. They wouldn't be doing anything more, even though the thought of abstaining was torturous enough. She was worth waiting for.

How ironic that the theme of today was survival, he mused, feeling the caffeine slowly render him ready for the day's lessons as the kids emerged slowly from their tents. As much as she'd made it clear that they could be there for each *other*, he felt as though all he was living for now was to make things good for Kaya and keep her safe from the world.

He rolled his eyes at himself. God, he was in trouble.

Survival and its various techniques were clearly a favourite subject for Arno, Kaya thought as the kids took furious notes and clamoured to be part of his hands-on demonstrations. She was listening in, buttering bread for lunch-time sandwiches.

'Breaking survival down to its basics, it's all about three life-saving elements: shelter, warmth, and water,' he was saying now. 'Without any of these, you'll fade fast in the wild before you can have any hope of rescue.'

It wasn't anything she didn't know but, even with her knowledge of first aid and emergency care, she wouldn't stand much chance here, without Arno around. It wasn't Amsterdam. The more she thought about that, the more she didn't want to go home so soon. Would he ask her to stay?

She smiled to herself, smothering peanut butter onto a slice, letting her mind wander. She couldn't stay, she'd already decided that, but she felt a little better, a little more in control of her life. Maybe it *was* possible to get out of her head, and just enjoy him.

It was the sexiest thing on earth watching Arno construct a shelter from sticks and stones with his bare hands, encouraging the kids to help. She couldn't get the image of their kiss in the rain from her head, or what had happened after, unfortunately, when she'd asked him to make love to her and he'd refused.

She cringed, catching his eye over the makeshift shelter.

'A shelter will protect you if the wind and cold or even the sun get too much,' he said, holding her gaze a second too long as he snapped a branch in his hands, sending her mind back to the seductive thrill of his fingers trailing the circumference of her navel, the sparks that had set her insides on fire the second his hands had cupped her breasts. She could still feel the length of him hardening between her legs.

She swallowed, realising Kimberley was grinning at her from her place, folding towels by the tents.

'The shelter will provide a vital element of protection in an otherwise desperate situation,' Arno told the group. 'If you're lost, the shelter will be your protective environment while you wait, whether it's hours or days or maybe weeks…'

Hours, days, weeks…

Kaya bit hard on her lip, stabbing a knife back into the peanut-butter jar. How long would she have to wait to feel him so close again? She didn't have much time, but he was right, she couldn't be rushed. Couldn't even rush herself, not when the slightest, stupidest shadow was enough to set her back.

'We'll need a fire next,' he was saying. 'Heat and flames can send a signal to potential rescuers.'

She was hot, without the fire, she realised, swiping at her clammy forehead. Just the memories from that tent, and the way he'd kissed her in the rain as though their lives depended on it, were enough to get her burning up.

In minutes, their little fire was crackling. Kimberley winked at her over a towel, bobbed her head suggestively towards Arno, and Kaya felt her face flush. Kimberley had heard her come back from Arno's tent this morning, but all she'd said was, 'Did you get lucky with the doctor?'

'Depends what you mean by lucky,' she'd replied. Lucky he didn't kick her out then and there for being a tease. Lucky he'd come back even after she'd tried to push him away.

'Does anyone know what we can add to that

fire, to make smoke?' he said, shoving his shirt sleeves higher up his arms, showcasing the snake with its fangs on his arm.

A flurry of hands shot up at his question and it sucker-punched her, the cold, hard fact that she was totally, irrevocably smitten. That stupid snake tattoo…maybe Mama Imka was onto something there. She didn't have to rush; like a snake, she could go slowly. He *had* been a gentleman. But if they went any slower now she'd scream.

'That's right,' he was saying, passing a bunch of green leaves to one of the girls. 'See what these do to the fire.'

The leaves sent a cloud of smoke high into the sky. The kids all clapped. The young girl beamed from under her sunhat as if she'd solved a riddle and scored a prize, and Kaya ran her eyes over his lips from afar, conjuring back the taste of him.

They hadn't even gone all the way, but the embarrassment of her little turn had faded now; she was more determined than ever to have him make love to her, at least once, before she had to go home. She'd always wonder if she didn't! So what if it made her miss him more, or she got attached? That was all called being alive, and being a woman. Finally, she was starting to feel like a woman again, thanks to him.

A chorus of *'Ew...'* and *'Gross...'* almost cancelled out the frogs in the river and she startled
from her thoughts, only to discover he'd explained that their own pee could also be used
on a fire to make smoke.

He sure knew everything there was to know
about fire.

Kaya frowned at the slice of bread before her
now. Did she get through to him at all, last night?

Mama Annika didn't blame him for that miscarriage, surely, the way she was always reaching out to him. He'd just taken his dad's words
to heart, even though the man was probably an
emotional mess at the time. She hadn't met him
but, judging by the love she'd felt in that home,
every scrap of Arno's guilt was unwarranted. If
he'd only talk to them both about it, instead of
making all these excuses not to be around them,
they'd have him shed that truckload of guilt in
no time...

Kimberley was calling her over from the tent.
Dropping her peanut-butter duties, she wandered
over.

'Help me with this one, will you?' she said,
gesturing to the end of a cotton tablecloth. 'I
can't believe how fast this weekend has gone
already!'

'Me neither,' Kaya said as the kids cheered at
something Arno said behind them.

'Is he as good to you as he is to them?' Kimberley pried, gesturing to him over the giant tablecloth. Kaya sighed. These days, she had no energy to even deny it.

'He's everything to me,' she admitted.

'Then snare him!'

CHAPTER EIGHTEEN

TODAY WAS THE DAY. Arno had already decided. It was less than a month now till Kaya and the rest of the volunteers were due to board their planes back to their respective countries. Usually he'd be excited to welcome a new group, but this was different. Time was ticking by too fast; he had to ask if she wanted to stay longer.

Just come out and ask her already!

He should have asked by now, he thought, finding her across the mud and grass that constituted Mama Imka's village's football pitch—where they'd set up their temporary medical centre for this afternoon's treatments. But he'd been trying to enjoy the moment. Every moment with her.

The weeks they'd spent together since that camping expedition were a blur that could bring a goofy smile to his face any time, anywhere. He'd shown her how to fire a gun, hit a moving target with a tranquilliser dart. She knew the names of the birds who sang in the new dawn, and at the top of Table Mountain he wished he had half his mama's skills, so he could paint her against the sunset, so he'd never have to stop looking at her face.

It was all new to him—a year with Bea hadn't even compared to the depth of his emotions now after just a few months, but if he asked her to stay and she refused him...

They hadn't even had that conversation—it was as if they'd both silently agreed to enjoy this for what it was, without worrying about the future, and the last thing he wanted was to pressure her.

Could he even commit to something serious, with someone so much younger, from an entirely different country? Could he keep her safe and protected long-term, as she deserved and needed?

That was the real issue that was keeping him up at night. He couldn't stand the thought of letting her down in any way.

'Mama Imka is ready for her medicine,' she said now, walking over to meet him in her uniform blue T-shirt. His eyes lingered on her hair, then the smooth caramel flesh on show inside the V of her collar. 'Do you want to do it, or shall I?'

She fiddled with her necklace suddenly and he sighed to himself, getting up from his seat, wishing just the sight of her didn't turn him on so much in public—a result of abstaining from sex all this time, he supposed. She'd got him so wound up, so utterly frustrated that no wonder his head was a carousel of questions around her.

'You don't want to?'

'I don't mind,' she lied, looking at the floor.

She was nervous being around Mama Imka, because of whatever she'd told her, or *predicted*, when she'd first arrived. Sometimes he wondered if she'd predicted something to do with *him*.

'You still haven't told me what she said to you,' he reminded her, crossing the grass with her, past the kids playing football, towards the hut.

'That's for me to know, and you to find out,' she said cryptically, but he didn't miss her gaze flickering to his forearm, where his tattoo was peeking from his shirt sleeve. He stopped, shoved his sleeve up and studied it, looking for a fly or a tick, or something.

'What?' he asked, confused.

She shook her head. 'Nothing. Why don't we both go in to her?'

'Deal,' he said.

'You know…' She paused. 'You haven't told me what she said to you, either. Before I even got here.'

'What makes you think it was about you?' he

teased, and he touched a hand to her back, to guide the way.

His touch seemed to stop her short in her tracks. Kaya crumpled his shirt sleeve up tightly in her hand and sighed so heavily through clenched lips she could have uprooted a tree. He could read her sighs by now. Kaya thought she was ready for more. She was chomping at the bit; probably more frustrated than him, but he'd refused her, over and over, and over.

Maybe he was crazy…but it was better than having her react badly and feeling as if he'd pressured her. Maybe he'd give into her, if she wanted to stay longer.

'How are we feeling today?' she chirruped as they entered the hut together. Kaya was clearly trying to appear indifferent in front of Mama Imka, he mused now. Her nerves made his pulse quicken; she was right, he hadn't ever told her about the real significance of their encounter in the sunflower garden. In truth he was still struggling with that one himself.

'Ah, the two of you together, what a delight.' Mama Imka looked worryingly pale today, and frailer than she had done even last week, when he'd come with one of the other volunteers.

'She has a cough, and chest pains,' her daughter croaked from the doorway. Then she lit three candles and Arno knew Kaya was thinking the same thing. The meds were just keeping her stable now. HIV and TB together had weakened her immune system; even the smallest illness or bug could wreak havoc on her fragile body.

'I'm fine,' Mama Imka insisted, before hacking into her hand.

'We may have to move you to the hospital,' he said gently, and the old woman tried her best to sit up, waving Kaya's hands away as she offered her another blanket.

'I'm not going anywhere,' she said, adamantly. 'I told you that, Dr Nkosi. This is where I belong.'

'But if you get worse, you won't have the help you need here,' Kaya tried as Arno prepared her medicine. The six-month course was almost up, and while she had good days and bad days, the bad days were catching up with her.

He felt Kaya's frustration as the woman insisted she wouldn't go, not even if she was at death's door. Then she insisted she was fine with death welcoming her, as it had done her husband several years ago.

'I don't know what to do, she's so stubborn,' Kaya told him outside, when they were packing up the Jeep. 'Are you sure the two of you aren't related?'

'Very funny,' he said. Then he saw the genuine concern on her face. 'Some people round here, especially from the small villages, don't put much faith in traditional medicine. They believe in…other things.'

She pouted, thoughtfully. 'We must be able to force her. She needs full-time care by professionals.'

'We can't force her to do anything,' he told her. 'I wish we could.'

'But she'll die here.'

'That's her choice.'

Kaya was silent. She climbed up into the Jeep with a jaded sigh, and he wished he could reassure her, but she didn't know how these things worked out here. It wasn't as if it were where she was from. There was a lot she still didn't know about life here. Not all of it was saving lives, most of it was just making it a little bit more comfortable.

He searched for something positive to tell her.

On the road, he almost let on about the plaque he'd finally had made in honour of his brother. The copper memorial had arrived just last week—*Remembering Baby Kung.* He was planning to present it to Mama Annika, and maybe even suggest they open the restaurant again. He would help, of course. It was time. But he was still procrastinating…it needed to be the right time. Kaya would tell him to drive there right now if he brought all this up. That was the problem. These were conversations he had to have with Mama *and* Dad, in private, especially after all this time.

Speak of the devil. His phone was ringing. They must have driven into range; the signal was so sporadic out here.

Swiping it from the dash, he answered on speakerphone. He knew better than to ignore her these days, and actually it felt pretty good to know that their mother-son relationship was slowly getting back on track; even if it was mostly small talk.

'Dinner, with you and Dad tonight?' he answered her now. 'Me and Kaya?'

Mama Annika wanted them to stay over, too, and he paused before answering. It was best not to refuse. His recent efforts to be a better son weren't going unnoticed, why refuse a nice dinner invitation?

How was she to know he'd been planning to take Kaya to dinner himself tonight, and ask her if she'd stay on, somewhere quiet where they wouldn't be interrupted?

'I'd love to,' Kaya said into the phone, much to his surprise. She had never met his dad before, and even though she'd insisted he probably didn't blame Arno for what happened to Mama, Arno had yet to talk to him about it. Their relationship had been based on small talk for so long he wasn't sure what they'd all find to say. Either way, Arno saw his plan fly straight out of the window.

Kaya hadn't quite been expecting the spitting image of Arno—an older, greyer version of him at least—to welcome them into the house and talk her ear off about the wine industry around the kitchen table, and now that she was here, something didn't feel right.

She realised, halfway through her plate of white bean casserole, that she'd accepted in anticipation of a very different introduction by Arno, especially as she was meeting his father, but he'd still called her his *volunteer*.

He reached for her fingers under the table the second her parents got up to fetch themselves more wine from the cellar. 'Sorry about him,' he said.

'I like hearing your father talk,' she said, releasing his fingers quickly, the second they walked back into the room.

He threw her a look she knew meant *What's wrong with you?* But she concentrated on her napkin. Maybe he was wondering why she was suddenly awkward, but the longer she was here, the more uncomfortable she was, not knowing what this *thing* was. If it was just a fling, should she really be here, getting to know his parents?

Where did she stand?

She shouldn't have come.

'I was kind of hoping we could talk tonight, somewhere else, alone,' he whispered now, while his parents discussed the vintage bottle excitedly, opposite them.

'Oh?' Kaya's heart sped up as the butterflies struck her belly. She was about to ask what about, when Mama Annika started talking about the restaurant, how she'd been thinking about opening it again, how a new hot chef had expressed interest, and what did Arno think? Could he help locate a structural engineer? Could they move the memorial there, where it really belonged?

Arno looked as though someone had just put a live cable into his bathtub. 'I was going to suggest the same thing, but, Mama, Dad, I think we all need to talk—'

'Maybe Kaya can plant us a little restaurant garden,' Mama said next, cutting him off in her excitement. 'How long do we have you for, lovely Kaya?'

Kaya's heart leapt up to her throat.

'I do hope you'll be back again to visit? Or maybe Arno can visit you in Holland?'

Arno sat back in his chair. Kaya waited again. Now might be a nice time for him to confirm that either suggestion would be nice, but he mumbled a non-committal *maybe*, staring at the blackened kitchen wall, drumming his fingers on the table.

Her stomach plummeted right through the bottom of her chair. Of course he wasn't going to visit her, he had far too much going on here… and now this. Not that she could blame him; she should be happy he seemed to be getting more involved with his family. It was what she wanted for him, but…

He threw her an apologetic look and she forced a smile, even as fear struck her like a thunderbolt. She'd been here before, she'd felt it, right before Pieter announced he was seeing Claudette and didn't love her any more.

'I have a few weeks left here yet,' she explained quickly, forcing an air of indifference she prayed they bought. 'My parents have planned a big welcome-home party already. The hospital where I work have asked for confirmation of a return date, so I guess it's all set.'

'You're going back to the hospital?' Arno's brow furrowed instantly next to her. She had his full attention, and a thrill darted through her as she straightened up. She'd told him Pieter's new girlfriend, Claudette—the one he cheated on her with—worked there. 'Is that a good idea?'

'It's a good opportunity.' She bristled. 'A promotion. No more night shifts.'

'I was hoping you might…' He trailed off, frowning at his plate while his parents looked between them in interest.

'Might what?' she pressed. Any second now, he would say it. He'd say he wanted her to stay, with the foundation, with this new restaurant launch, whatever that might involve. With him.

'I think he wants you to stay,' Mama Annika cut in with a grin at his dad, and Arno blew air through his lips, dragged a hand across his head.

'Mama!'

Kaya's cheeks flamed. Talk about putting them on the spot. She wanted to hear that from him, not them. And he hadn't said a word about it, much as he wasn't now. Gosh, she was an idiot.

'Well, I'm afraid I can't stay,' she forced herself to say firmly as her heart convulsed in her chest. 'Even though I do love…' she glanced at Arno '…love…it here, I have a lot going on back home.'

Excusing herself, she hurried to the bathroom, splashed cold water on her face and scolded herself in the mirror for her tears. She was here to grow a backbone, not crumble over a man.

The rest of the evening was torture.

Arno—even quieter than usual—tried to put his arms around her in the bedroom, and this time, for the first time ever, she removed herself from his embrace, told him she was too hot and needed a proper rest. He didn't argue. Didn't ask why she wasn't trying to throw herself on him as usual. Maybe, all things considered, he was glad she was backing off.

Eventually, in the darkness, he said, 'Are you really going back to that hospital?'

'Is that all you want to say?' she snapped, annoyance getting the better of her.

He was silent for a long time. 'I don't know what to say, Kaya. I know your life is somewhere else. And mine is here; it will always be here.'

He sounded sad, and her heart broke into a million pieces. 'I know,' she said again, forcing her voice not to shake. 'It is what it is, Arno, we both knew that, going in.'

Lying with her back to him in the tension, Kaya cursed her stupidity. She should have known this would happen. That she'd fall hook, line and sinker, only to be left in a pile of wreckage. No wonder he wouldn't sleep with her. For a second, back there at the table, she'd thought by 'talk' he'd meant something else, because she'd been dying for him for weeks. He'd been fending her off, as if he was afraid he might break her if they tried again, and it was getting to be intolerable. Now, she was starting to understand.

He'd been here for her, as he'd said he would, but as for wanting to see her after this… That was all just wishful thinking in a moment of passion and wrought emotion. He was already anticipating her departure. He'd accepted they were far too different for this to be anything real and lasting. It was time she did the same.

Arno Nkosi was enough of a gentleman that he wouldn't just sleep with her and abandon ship, not after what she'd been through, but as for wanting anything more than a temporary fling, well… This was not her own parents' love story. This was her own, and it was not going to have a happy ending.

CHAPTER NINETEEN

TANDE WASN'T AT the gates, waiting for him at sunrise as she usually was. Arno couldn't help but see it as an omen. It was never going to be a great day—the day Kaya was leaving.

The morning round was perfunctory at best, just himself and Mark: a spate of jabs, some meds to be administered, one fractured wrist. He stopped by the village to check on a withering but steadfast and stubborn Mama Imka, took a few Polaroid shots of the blossoming sunflowers and plump beans that were almost ready for picking in the veggie garden. Kaya might like to take them home.

It wasn't exactly the parting gift he'd had in mind for her, but with things the way they were she hadn't really given him much time or attention since they'd left the winery that night. Switched off might be the better term, and his own self-preservation had drawn a deeper line between them.

She was leaving today.

He drove back to Thabisa slowly, watching the clouds make faces at him over the mountains.

That night had been driving him crazy ever since. So much for getting her alone, to talk to her. First his father had talked her ear off, which had surprised him—he hadn't brought anyone home in so long he'd clean forgotten how they both still thrived amongst company. Then Mama had thrown a bombshell about wanting to reopen the restaurant. His words had got all tangled.

He had been about to just come out and say it, right there in front of Kaya and Dad too—that he was sorry he hadn't been strong enough for her up till now, sorry about not being there when she needed him that night, and all the years after, sorry for waiting so long to give her the damn plaque. It had been right there in the Jeep, waiting for him to hand it over.

Then Kaya had announced she was going. Everything he'd been building up in his head had just flown out of the window.

She was so sure about it. Even about going back to the hospital. She had a life back home that didn't involve him, and he had one here. The whole time he'd been thinking of asking her to stay, she was already accepting a new job in Amsterdam!

He wasn't about to try and pressure her into

anything. That wasn't the way to handle her. So that was it. It had been fun. More than fun. The best thing that had ever happened to him, even without the sex, and that was something he'd never thought he'd say.

Now he just had to suck it up and put it in the past. Somehow, he had to say goodbye.

By the time he returned to Thabisa, the farewell cocktails were well under way. He slunk past the group, catching Kaya's eye briefly. The long, lingering look she gave him twisted a knot in his stomach, which stuck the whole time he was showering and changing. He sat in a towel on the bed, pulled out the best Polaroid to give her. Picking up a pen, he hovered it over the back.

Should he?

Well, at this point he had nothing to lose.

He wrote on the back, kept it brief, kept it neat.

Then he changed his mind. He couldn't give her this! It would mess with her head; she'd made a decision. Who was he to stand in her way? She deserved more anyway…someone who at least knew how to look after a woman.

Standing, he felt the fury at himself grown tenfold. The plaque taunted him from the dresser. He hadn't even faced his own parents yet. It had been nothing but excuses. Enough was enough. Grabbing it up, he swiped the Jeep keys and drove like a bat out of hell to the estate. He'd be back before the group left, but he was damned if he'd put this conversation off one moment longer. Yes, he'd let Kaya slip through his fingers, but he was still his mother's only son.

'Where's Arno?'

Kimberley went to hand her another drink but Kaya refused it, eyes scanning the forecourt. The bus would be arriving to take them to Cape Town in less than an hour, and she was starting to worry he wouldn't even say goodbye.

'I don't know,' she admitted as her pulse spiked. Around her, the volunteers were laughing, toasting a job well done, talking excitedly about plans for home, but she was worried. OK, so they'd cooled things off, but it wasn't like him to just disappear.

'What happened with you two?' Kimberley asked her again. She'd been asking for days but Kaya wasn't sharing. She didn't really know herself. Nothing, she supposed. They'd slipped right back to being colleagues since that night at the winery and she assumed that was fine by him. It was for the best, all things considered, but to not even say goodbye?

Now she was just…angry.

Excusing herself, she walked to his room, stood at the bottom of the porch steps. The lights were off inside, but what if he was in there? Anxiety gnawed at her insides. What if he was sick?

'Arno?' The door opened in front of her right as she knocked, and she braced herself. But he didn't answer. He'd just left his door unlocked.

She stepped inside, looked around for the Jeep keys. If those were gone, she'd know he'd driven somewhere himself. The room smelled of him, his unmistakeable scent. Weakened by what she'd lost, she stopped and caught her breath. She'd got so used to his scent in her nostrils, and the time she'd spent without it lately had felt empty, bland, boring, but what was she supposed to do?

'Where are you?' she growled as emotion rose in her and threatened to consume her. Then… what was that?

Sinking to the bed, she picked up what looked like a postcard. No, a Polaroid. Her hand flew over her mouth. It was a photo of the vegetable garden, and three sunflowers. They must have just come up this week, from the seeds she'd planted.

When did he take this? Why did he leave it here?

There was writing on the back. Kaya's hands trembled as she read it. Suddenly, she was struggling for breath.

Kaya,

Mama Imka told me a great love would bloom with the sunflowers. She was right.
I think I'll love you for ever.
Arno x

Kaya swiped at her eyes. This was not happening!

How on earth was this real? Not just the prediction about the sunflowers, but him writing *I think I'll love you for ever*.

He had never told her that. Why hadn't he told her?

'Kaya, are you here?' She sprang from the bed at the voice outside. Kimberley was racing up the porch steps. 'Where's Arno?'

'I don't know,' she said again. 'He's not here, his keys aren't here!'

Kimberley looked frightened suddenly. 'When did you last see him?'

'An hour ago, I'm not sure, I was outside with you, I just saw him pass by, and now he's gone again. What's happened?'

Dread pulsed through her. Kimberley's face wasn't helping. 'There's been some kind of attack,' Kimberley said, panting in the doorway. 'They found a man. He's unrecognisable, they said. It just came through on the radio. They think it was a lion. You don't think it's... Tande?'

* * *

A tear-stained Mama Annika, in her paint-splattered kaftan, loved the plaque. She hugged Arno closer than he'd let her get in years and put it straight on the wall by the kitchen door. When Dad walked in, his words got caught in his throat, but he forced them out.

'I always thought you blamed me for what happened to Kung. So I blamed myself, all this time.'

His father pulled him into him, along with Mama. They stood there for what felt like for ever while Dad told him what Kaya had: that he'd spoken from the pain and loss and anger at *himself* for not being there either, and had in no way intended for Arno to carry the blame.

'I should have been there for you that night, Mama. Dad was right about that.'

'We're so proud of you, son. You took what happened that night and you turned it around. Look at all the lives you save now.'

Mama would have none of his apologies for the years he felt as if he'd shut her out. All she had ever wanted was for him to be happy. It was as if he'd shed a blanket made of concrete on the kitchen floor.

Relief flooded through him in the arms of his family, right before he remembered he'd just lost as much as he'd gained.

Mama asked him, 'Isn't Kaya leaving today?'

'She's all packed up.'

Mama Annika gasped and started ushering him out of the door. 'Go, go! I thought you would ask her to stay longer!'

He tried to explain. 'You heard her. She has a life to get back to.'

Mama Annika just crossed her arms and closed her eyes, and shook her head at her feet, and he knew then, he'd really messed it up.

'Son, you need to learn a few things about us women. She was waiting for you to show her you want her! Go get her. That is an order.'

Arno didn't need telling twice. Already he could feel the concrete blanket was back around his shoulders, thinking it was too late. She might already be on that bus, to Cape Town.

Kissing Mama goodbye and shaking his father's hand with a promise to be back soon to take a look at the restaurant plans, he sped back to the Jeep, only to find his radio buzzing off the hook.

An emergency, something to do with a lion, a man…an attack. Bashing the co-ordinates into the satnav and praying to God this wasn't the reason why he hadn't seen Tande today, he roared out of the driveway, checking the time. He'd go straight to the airport after this—he'd go get Kaya. Or at least tell her how much she'd changed his life.

Because of her, he might actually have a great relationship with Mama *and* Dad going forward. Because of her, he'd at least shed the guilt of being someone who couldn't protect what was his. He'd done all he could at the time. Mama had even said, *'If you hadn't dragged me out, I'd be dead too!'*

The body, when he got to it, no longer even looked like a human. A village of people were crowded round, panicking, screaming. 'It went that way, the lion went that way!'

Arno's heart bucked. What if it *was* Tande? Something could have happened…anyone might provoke her.

The pathway through the mountains was overgrown jungle, but there was a village at the end of it. One that would have no idea a lion might be heading for them.

Arno gathered his gun and tranquilliser darts from the Jeep and sprinted into the bush.

The emergency rescue vehicle, with just herself and two male staff members from Thabisa, was speeding down the gravel road. Kaya's butt should be bruised and sore from the lack of suspension in the back, but she barely felt it. No one could reach Arno.

His radio seemed to be out of range. Someone had seen him at the scene of the attack; they said he'd gone off alone into the mountains. Probably looking for Tande.

Somewhere ahead, a plane soared over the mountains. Maybe it was hers, she didn't care. The others had left once they knew the person who'd been mauled wasn't Arno, but she'd hugged Kimberley goodbye and joined the rescue crew. It had been four hours now, and there was still no sign of him. Gut-wrenching loss made a mess of her make-up; her heart felt as if it might explode.

The conversation around the dining table played out again in her head as she scanned the roadside for him, the siren blaring. She'd thought about that night a million times since, but now she could see it so differently.

He'd been dealing with his parents coming at him about reopening that restaurant; that would have been a tough subject for him, all things considered. And she'd only thought about *herself* in that moment, read him all wrong. All she'd done was panic and project her stupid fears of rejection onto him, made him think she didn't even want to be there, or with him.

And now he was gone…possibly in the wilderness with a lion that might or might not be Tande. Mikal had confirmed they hadn't seen Tande all day—maybe she had escaped and got hungry. Kaya couldn't even entertain the thought that

Tande would do something like that, let alone to Arno…

'I see something.' Their driver pulled the vehicle to a stop. Sure enough, she could see something flickering, a torch, maybe. They'd come a different way from the route the guys at the scene said he'd taken on foot, and now they were stopped at the entry point to what must be the most remote village she'd ever seen. The pathway was so narrow, they couldn't drive it. She leapt from the vehicle and didn't even flinch when Mikal tried to grab her wrist to hold her back.

'Be careful!'

He was right. Kaya drew a deep breath, quoting herself on the outdoor expedition: *First do no harm…you'll be more help if you just stay calm.* She took the tranquilliser gun from the door and shoved it into her belt with a purpose, swallowing down her galloping heart.

Then, she ran for the light, swiping the bushes as they lunged for her, and only stopped dead when a deafening roar ahead splintered her senses.

CHAPTER TWENTY

THE LION'S ROAR could have started an avalanche and Arno's heart was a freight train as he motioned for the mother and her two small children across the small clearing to stay quiet.

'Where are you, buddy?' he whispered to the beast, scanning the shadows. It was close, judging by that sound.

The woman held her kids close, huddled in a doorway to one of three tiny huts, pitched around a campfire. The men, they said, had gone to another village for supplies, and left them with no gun, but the hunk of animal meat on the spit above the fire must have lured the predator close.

Just then, a crack of a branch ten feet away sent his pulse roaring louder than the lion. 'Get inside,' he told the cowering woman, poised with one hand on his holster.

It wasn't a lion that emerged slowly from the bush, clutching a gun with two hands. It was

Kaya. Mikal was close behind her. 'What are you doing here?' he snapped. 'It's dangerous!'

'Looking for you,' she said, and in less than a second flat she'd sprinted across the circle, past the fire, to his side. She was panting heavily, her dress was crumpled, her forehead clammy. She was supposed to be on a plane! For a moment he was totally thrown.

'Are you crazy?' he said, coming to his senses, just as Mikal's voice echoed out in the night.

'Arno, watch out!'

He darted in front of Kaya as the two kids screamed and shrieked from the doorway. A giant lion, almost the size of his Jeep, pounced from the roof of one of the huts and landed with a thwack on the dirt between them, its huge paws less than six feet away from Arno's toes.

'Don't move,' he said.

Across the circle, Mikal pointed the gun as the lion stalked the slab of meat in the firelight, shaking his mane. Kaya's breathing was a ragged scratch behind him and he wanted to yell at her for putting herself in danger, for making him responsible for her. Because his heart quite literally would not handle it if anything happened… But she'd come for him. Instead of getting on that plane.

One of the kids sniffed, and the lion looked up, seemingly turning his attention to a new target.

'Not the kid,' Kaya cried now, going to step out from behind him. The movement made the lion spin and take a new aim. Right at them.

Arno drew a breath, then loaded a dart. Neither of them made a sound. Its black eyes glimmered in the firelight. Time slowed to nothing, then a surge of fury took a hold of him. There was no way in hell he was letting any harm come to Kaya, or anyone here!

'Want me to shoot?' Mikal was poised.

'I'll do it,' he said.

One finger on the trigger, he made his body a shield for Kaya. He hated to shoot, even with a tranquilliser, more than anything, but if he didn't have a choice...

Just then, another rustle in the bushes drew the lion's gaze away, and before Arno could quite tell what was happening, another big cat was on top of their stalker, wrestling the lion to the ground.

'Tande!' Kaya grabbed his arm. He made quick work while the cats were distracted and backed with her around the fire, away from the wrestling match. Screaming kids pierced his ears as the family of three ran to Mikal. Arno told him not to shoot.

Tande must have heard them and come to his rescue. His usually gentle lioness was biting and clawing and scratching her way to victory, until, as quickly as she'd arrived, she'd shooed the giant lion off, sent it packing the way it had come. They watched from the ground as it leapt, defeated, back onto the roof with a growl and darted off into the night.

They were left there, breathless, while Tande helped herself to the meat around the fire, lounging on the ground with it between her paws, like a contented cat.

'Unreal,' Kaya whispered, dropping her gun to the ground and turning to him. 'What just happened?'

He cupped her beautiful face in his damp hands, and kissed her before he could even think, half in relief, half in desire, mostly in desire— she'd never looked better. She kissed him back, deeply, hungrily, told him sorry, over and over and over.

'I saw the photo you took, on your bed,' she said after a moment, searching his eyes. 'I went looking for you when you didn't come say goodbye. Why didn't you tell me?'

'Tell you what?' he asked her, smoothing her cheeks. He could hardly believe she was still here, or indeed what had just happened. It could have turned out a completely different story. His brain wasn't working.

'That you think you'll love me for ever,' she said, taking his hand, pressing it to her heart. 'You've changed everything, Arno. I shouldn't have ever made you think I didn't want more than… I just got caught up in my own head. I didn't want you to end things first. You wouldn't sleep with me…'

'I had my own stuff going on in my own stupid head,' he replied with a wry laugh, and she kissed him again. God, he'd missed these lips, the feel of her hair tickling his face, her eyes. 'And you have no idea how it killed me, not sleeping with you.'

She bit her lip, looked up through her eyelashes. 'What do we do now? I missed my flight.'

'You can keep on missing flights,' he told her, taking her hands, then claiming her mouth again with his. In truth, he had no idea what was next, except the bedroom, but as long as she was looking at him like this, and kissing him like this, he knew they would work it out.

EPILOGUE

One year later

'MY PARENTS ARE obsessed with you,' Kaya exclaimed as they left the house on Kerkstraat and made their way across Leidseplein towards the canal.

'Well, who wouldn't be?' Arno joked, bringing her hand to his mouth and placing a light kiss on her fingers.

'I'm serious. I think my mum's reliving her childhood there, through you. They're going to want to come and stay longer next time.'

'They're welcome to,' he said, and Kaya's heart swelled to the size of a watermelon as they strolled hand in hand in the twilight, stopping while she acted like a proud tour guide for Arno. He was seeing Amsterdam at its absolute best today, right before sunset, when the sky was streaked red and golden, as it often was in South Africa.

Her parents had stayed there for a whole month last time, half at Thabisa for safaris, half at Nkosi Valley. They had even helped pick tomatoes and leeks, and plant more seeds in the Mama Imka Memorial Garden, which had strangely blossomed beyond belief since they had lost her, seven months ago.

Their mothers had acted like long-lost friends, so much so that she and Arno had often left them to chatter for hours, while they had gone and done...other things.

They were pretty good at the other things, she thought now as a tram rumbled past and someone on it eyed up Arno as if he were a hunk of meat. She didn't mind; it was nice to be the one who'd snared him, as Kimberley said.

He'd been patient. More patient than her.

'Your mama's a great cook,' he said now, patting his full stomach and guiding her across the street, towards the park. 'She should talk to Mama Annika again, put a Dutch dish on the restaurant menu when it opens next month.'

'Mmm...' she said, though now she was distracted. She could see the treetops from here over the chocolate-box houses and a fluttering in her belly tried to warn her, this was not where she wanted to be. Arno didn't know that.

She held his hand tighter, trying not to think

about it. Usually she wouldn't walk this way. But this was Arno's first time, meeting her family on home turf, seeing the city she'd left behind to move to South Africa and be with him. He deserved to see the park—it was beautiful. A city highlight. At least, he could see the outside of it.

He stopped with her at the tall, wrought-iron gates, letting the cyclists hurry past them into the park, as if sensing her apprehension. 'I know you don't like this place,' he said softly. 'Your mother told me it was here but...'

Kaya took a deep breath, then released it through her mouth, right before he kissed her. 'Trust me,' he said, and his warm eyes steadied her heart. Of course she trusted him.

But... Oh...

What was he doing...dropping to the floor... getting his jeans all dirty...going down on his knees? On *one* knee.

Oh, my God.

Her hands flew to her mouth, right as the tears sprang to her eyes and almost blurred the moment from her vision. The box, the ring. 'Are you serious, Arno?'

'Marry me,' he said now.

'Yes!' she cried as he slid the silver studded band from the velvet clasp onto her finger, where she knew she would never, ever take it off.

He picked her up as if she were a weightless feather and spun her around, making several people stop on their bikes and cheer.

'I love you,' she breathed into his neck, wrapping her arms around him, and the crowd of clapping strangers grew around them as they kissed for what should have been an embarrassingly long time. They were almost deafening in their support. Suddenly this was not the same park—only *good* things happened here.

'Let's go inside,' she said a moment later, surprising herself. Never in a million years did she think she'd be suggesting this.

'Are you sure?' Arno smoothed her hair, and took her hand, admiring the ring on it.

'I'm sure, now you're with me,' she assured him. 'What can happen?'

The park was as beautiful as she remembered. They stopped at the pond, where the ducks left their trails in the water. Took photos by the sculpture shaped like a fish and watched the joggers and the dogs run around. He led her to a bench by the rose garden where they sat with her head on his shoulder, watching the world go by. The scent of the petals and the jasmine bushes tickled her nostrils and as Arno kissed the top of her head she felt complete, and free of fear for the first time in years, maybe ever.

Arno was the best person to be here with; no one could hurt her while he was at her side, not here or anywhere.

* * * * *

If you enjoyed this story, check out these other great reads from Becky Wicks

Highland Fling with Her Best Friend
The Vet's Escape to Paradise
A Princess in Naples
White Christmas with Her Millionaire Doc

All available now!